The Halting Problem

The Halting Problem

Jeffrey Cohlmeyer

Chapter One

Welcome to The Noog

The millennial stared at me puzzled.

I skulked, then went back to my desk.

Now, I know that these younger types know very little about older science fiction movies, but for the work we do here, how can you not have seen it? Or even heard of it? I think they even did a gritty reboot of it a few years ago.

And the actor. My goodness. To date, he is the biggest grossing actor of all time. I think they had to invent a number to calculate his worldwide gross. Yet the millennial sat there, still puzzled, and started to fidget awkwardly as I made up my mouth to continue on this path of conversation.

But I stopped. I pursed my lips and stopped to think. The millennial, exhibiting that touch of class and patience his generation are known for, went back to staring at his phone, slack-jawed and dead-eyed.

Of course I could plumb the depths of my own *out-of-touched-ness* by quizzing this nerd. We've been down that road many times. It always gets to the point he utters something along the lines of:

"Oh, yeah, I've heard of him. He's the old guy from the oOpy commercial...you know, oOpy, the smartphone app I use to Bluetooth my phone to my cat's litterbox to activate the coffeemaker when I need to have my mom come over and do my laundry."

I decided that conversation would be, at best, pointless, at worst, homicidal. My total body count for the day was zero, and it really should stay that way if I ever want to get a promotion.

Instead, I would take matters into my own hands and do what we "old timers" do: tattletale like grade schoolers. I went immediately to the one man who could resolve this matter once and for all: my boss, Jack. Now, Jack is 12 years younger than me, so technically a millennial, but he knows his stuff, so that makes him an honorary non-millennial. We're planning an award ceremony for later in the year. He'll get a certificate, give a speech, that kind of stuff.

I like Jack. He started out at a time when most of the people working in tech were Generation X kids, like me, who grew up having to learn how to actually do things manually (I can still remember how difficult it was to go to the library and find a book using the Dewey Decimal System, for instance). But Jack still had that annoying optimism that all the millennials seem to have, and it served him well enough to earn promotions that older, cynical jerks like me earned but never got. Instead, we jerks got the stock options that always seemed to vest just after the company filed for bankruptcy.

It wasn't Jack's fault that he got promoted ahead of people like me. Or maybe it was, I don't know, but even so, I respected him for it. But the millennial was his hire, so that was all on him. And both of them must pay.

I playfully stormed into Jack's office, wearing a fake angry scowl to mask the actual scowl I had seconds ago. I was not sure if I could still pull this off. Everyone tells me I am a terrible liar.

Jack stared at me. I paused dramatically, desperately making it look like I was not trying to crack a smile. I mustered the fakest sounding angry voice I could under the circumstances.

"I want the millennial fired," I said.

"What? Why? Klaydin is one of our top recruits. He's a reliable operator. And, you don't know this...but he's a ninja."

"A ninja?" I was momentarily impressed, as my mind flashed back to older movies and cartoons from my youth.

"Yeah, a Javascript Ninja." Oh, it was millennial BS. Jack continued, "It says so on each of his five social media pages."

I took to social media like a giraffe to quicksand. "A five-page ninja?"

The fact that Jack seemed to buy any of this surprised me. I have never seen the millennial wear anything remotely cool enough to be considered "ninja."

Actually, come to think of it, I don't think I have even seen him wear anything black. All nut-crushing pants and anime hats. And, think about it. Real ninjas are stealthy. There is nothing stealthy about letting the entire planet know about you or your skillset on five social media websites. That would be the opposite of ninja, if such a word existed. That would be *anti-ninja*. A real ninja who knew how to program in Javascript would, I assume, use it in the dark somewhere, and they wouldn't have a damned cartoon doll hat on when they did it.

There had to be a law against misuse of that word. If anything, advertising yourself as a "(blank) ninja" should result in actual ninjas killing you, if for no other reason than to protect the brand name and image rights.

As I mulled this line of thinking over more, my real scowl started to creep out. I informed Jack of what movie the millennial had been oblivious to. Jack blinked, then raised an eyebrow suspiciously. I could tell he thought it was odd too, but needed more cajoling.

I doubled down. It was my only chance. "I don't care what dojo this loser stealthily escaped from. How can you let this punk kid work on the team after this? The whole GAI field is modeled after the concepts in that movie for god's sake!"

Jack laughed, but from the way he came down off his laugh, I could tell he was not going to fire this kid. "Brett, I don't really have time for your BS right now. We're on deadline and the last thing we need is a ninja cull."

While funny, I could not afford to laugh. I harrumphed, like a character in some movie too old for even me to remember the name of, and went back to my office down the hall. As I walked past the lab, I softly muttered "dagnabbit," both for effect and to soothe my shattered ego.

I shut the door to my office, and sighed. My desk was piled with file folders, memos and printed out email copies. This almost felt like a normal office when we're on deadline. Why were we on deadline? I have my suspicions. We have a meeting on Friday, but deadlines are just not used here. Training General Artificial Intelligence takes time to do it right.

I asked Jack about the deadline thing. He doesn't know either. Or he does but isn't telling me. I am not sure which would be worse.

I started to attack the paper stacks on my desk, but I caught myself glancing over at the millennial, who was in the lab, holding his phone three inches from his face. I stared at him for what had to be a solid minute, as he stared at the phone. His cheeks were reflecting the pale blue light from whatever he was watching. I think he blinked once. I was thankful that he at least was not wearing the virtual reality helmet attachment for his phone. He looks like an idiot when he does, and it embarrasses us all when people come to the office and see him watching 10 hour cat videos with what looks like a fairy's biker helmet on. You know, because seeing a cat jump on a coffee table and fall down is somehow not as funny unless it is in super hi-definition virtual reality, with the screen scratching your eyeballs.

And he had a way of making the place more his than someone his age should. Today, it was his doll. I know they call these things "plushes" now, but it's a doll. Does it have furry arms, big eyes, and is cuddly when you hug it? Is it for someone under the age of 8? Then it's a DOLL.

He had placed his yellow doll on the computer monitor in the lab. The lab was not his desk, but he thought he could just do that, like we would all accept having a bunch of toys around like it's Christmas. It's not Christmas; it's June. And even if it was Christmas, it's certainly not how we do Christmas here. We're adults, Christmas is supposed to suck for us.

4

He had this doll when he was a kid, and, as he lovingly told all of us, it has been with him ever since. I think he still lives with his mommy, so I'm not sure when the doll would have had a chance to get lost. He spoke about this doll like it was a living thing, like a baby or a pet hamster. And now, it was staring at me, mockingly. The desire to beat him senseless with it was overwhelming.

***

My name is Brett Phillips. As you may have guessed, I happily work in Artificial Intelligence.

The name of my company? I would tell you, but we have Non-Disclosure Agreements (NDAs) and at least one of our investors is trigger-happy with a lawsuit. But it is not like it matters anyway. We are a very small company you have never heard of in Chattanooga, Tennessee. We have about thirty employees at any time, depending on the time of year, but only three of us work with the program. We're called operators.

Why Chattanooga, of all places? Why not Silicon Valley? Why not New York City? *The Gig* is why. Chattanooga is one of the few places worth living in the continental US with excellent municipal broadband, and it just so happens to have the fastest internet service in the western hemisphere. Here, we call it *The Gig,* because we get 10 gbps when online, down and up. That's fast. Even on a slow day we get 950 mbps download speeds, and because the fiber optic lines are routed through the electric grid, we have virtually no downtime.

And, the program. My company is in the final stages of developing a program called *Pixie,* which is a General Artificial Intelligence (GAI) program. I can tell you the name *Pixie* because that is just what we call it internally to train it. Whatever businesses end up using her will change the name, probably to something stupid, then repurpose it to do whatever. Although, the mere thought of *Pixie* calling to sell you life insurance, for example, would be harrowing. Or calling her something stupid like *oOpy.*

Pixie is not the only GAI project going on for sure, but it is one of the best funded independent operations, so we have staff and resources available that smaller teams or less-financially stable developers would envy. Not that I am a name-dropper, but our principal investor is someone you have probably heard of: Troy Griffin. Yes, that Troy Griffin, the one you see on TV, hear on public radio, watch giving speeches and interviews online, and read about donating to charity. Not that I know him very well. He largely just gives us money piles to do one of his many vanity projects and occasionally gives an interview taking credit for all the work we do. Most of his time is spent in New York, from what I understand. He occasionally comes out for board meetings, but I have never actually talked to him. I did see him with Jack once, though.

And what do we do here? We do machine learning the right way.

In order to understand what I do and why we're the best, you have to understand AI in principle. Basically, there are two ways of developing AI.

The first way:

You can create oblivious robots that behave only in a certain, limited way over and over.

I know. Sounds nice but means nothing to you, right? An example may be helpful. Think of an automatic car wash. The arms, brushes, and sprays all work together to accomplish a task. The parts are not aware of what they are doing. They are not conscious like we are. They are programmed to do a simple list of tasks when ordered to do so. When you pull into the car wash, swipe your card, and drive over the sensors, you are effectively ordering it to execute its simple program.

However, this type of AI must operate in a completely controlled, "sandbox" environment to be effective. You enter the car wash, the door shuts, the machines go to work, and you leave with a clean car.

But if you try to apply "dumb" AI to the world as it is, it won't work...which makes sense if you think about it. Imagine if you tried to wash your car like an automatic car wash.

6

"Okay honey, tie the blue brushes around me and shove the pressure washer between my legs, I'm going to start spinning now."

When you can control the environment of the stupid robot, it can accomplish amazing things. But if you take the stupid robot into our world, it cannot work as intended. It would not survive. It would only do what it was programmed to do, then someone would come around and mercifully shut it off.

As a developer in this field, I have to be aware of this type of thing, and it is truly amazing when you consider the scope and breadth of what human ingenuity has accomplished with these dumb robots.

But, as with any amazing thing, the general public quickly becomes bored with it. Don't believe me? Ever marvel at an automatic car wash? Not since you were a kid, right?

This phenomenon is common across the entire human experience. The amazing becomes normal, and the normal becomes boring. Another example may help. Ask yourself how little you care about ginger. The spice, ginger. See, you did not even know what I was talking about.

Now, I know you have some ginger in your spice rack. Go look in your cabinet right now. You buy it once every 4 years, and always forget to add it to whatever you're cooking. What does it even go with? Can you put ginger in spaghetti? No? Then why do I have this?

But now, understand that humans hundreds of years ago happily *murdered* other humans for access to ginger. They really hated bland food, I guess. So, in honor of our dead ancestors who died for king and country in the glorious Spice Wars, ginger spice, along with sesame oil and soy sauce, goes very well with chicken breast if you are making Chicken Lo Mein.

The second way of looking at AI:

You can create generalist machines capable of operating in the world as it is, and gift them with human-like capabilities of thought, consciousness, and the ability to distinguish objects from the environment.

This type of AI is more in line with what the general public thinks of when they hear the term "Artificial Intelligence." Often, it comes in the form of killer robots and a dystopian future. But, as appealing as murderous, rampaging robots are in books and movies, the actual job of training these robots to act like humans is quite interesting.

As I quickly found out, luckily for the millennial, it is less murder and enslavement, more coordinating and studying. We utilize a framework for machine learning called a *neural network*. It is essentially a digital recreation of how the human mind learns. The GAI program learns by input, then analyzes the input, synthesizes data points, and always moves forward.

***

I fell into this field almost by accident.

I went to some non-prestigious college I am too embarrassed to mention in print and majored in Computer Science, a degree so embarrassingly vague that I laugh at the thought of anyone using a degree like that nowadays and getting a job with it. And as if that wasn't bad enough, my minor was Political Science. What can I say, it was the 1990s. All of my idiot advisors said it was good idea.

I am 47 now, but this was back at a time when computer programming jobs came with lame titles like "webmaster" and involved running a single flat page with HTML and several hundred dead hyperlinks on the bottom of the page. If you could press the power button on a computer and magically make company logos and mission statements appear on the internet, Baby Boomers would throw money at you. I still remember the guy who paid me $250.00 to put a dancing baby on his website. It took me longer to drive over to his office than to actually do it.

Sadly, though, the easy work dried up. As the big tech companies dumbed things down, the general public started understanding computers more. Gone were the days of having to know how to type three hundred lines of code into a command prompt in order to launch a spreadsheet. Along came what I call the *Push One Big Button* (*POBB*) applications. Internet search algorithms became so adept at figuring you out that you just had to *approximate* what you needed to know and it would give you the goods. Essentially, any moron who could point at or near something on a screen and not misspell a word too bad had the power of the personal computer in their grasp.

The result of all this simplification was that the Baby Boomers became a bit more computer savvy, and that was followed by a younger generation raised by these machines, so they had some skills. And of course, since I am disturbingly hyper-competitive, I had to work harder than them and expand my knowledge base to stay better than them. You never know which Javascript ninja is going to sneak up on you and *sai* your anus. So I always had work, but was always playing catch up to someone's kid, nephew, cousin, or mistress. In order to stay around and be relevant, I had to be the one who knew how to do things and, more importantly, would actually sit down and do them.

At no point was I ever drawn to AI as a legitimate field of employment. It always seemed like some futuristic dream, like I would go into the business of building universes or history eraser buttons. Ideally, yes, humanity should be pushing the envelope of what science tells us is impossible or really hard. GAI would certainly fall into that category.

In the real world, though, research and development flows from the people with the money to the people with the skill, and the people with the money want more money more than anything else. If some billionaire wants to have a smartphone app that sells school paste to non-profits in Uganda because he thinks he can double his money, he ponies up the $30,000,000.00, people like me get to work, and the cancer research has to wait.

So imagine my surprise when a former colleague of mine, Jack, contacted me and offered to fly me out to Chattanooga for an interview.

The story Jack told me was that he worked with a well-known angel investor, who in turn knew other investors, who all had wanted to fund a GAI project to do…something vague. Jack was a talker, and he was blabbering stuff about humanity and freedom. He sounded more politician than project manager. While he was giving his stump speech, all I could think of was cyborgs murdering millions of humans and enslaving the rest...you know, like a typical stump speech nowadays. I took Jack's call expecting Ugandan paste, and I got Death Robot 9000.

I spaced out. The opportunity to develop GAI, killer robots or not, along with Jack's ability to talk himself into explaining something eight different ways without mentioning any new information, sent me off into fantasyland.

Jack was oblivious, I think. There I was, sitting at a desk in some cubicle, in a Post-Industrial Michigan wasteland, copy-pasting some legacy code for some terrible plumber's website, and Jack thinks I need to be sold on this? Has Jack ever been to Michigan?

I waited for him to stop talking.

I took a deep breath, trying not to sound like I was going to jump through the phone to kiss him on the lips.

"When can I come out?"

Chapter Two

An Equitable Division of Labor is Best

Michigan is cold. You don't understand how relentlessly cold it is until you live there. Yes, I know you have experienced cold weather. Yes, I know you've seen ice storms. Yes, I know you were once kidnapped, stripped naked, and left for dead in Alaska. But all I am saying is that what makes Michigan winters so depressingly godawful is the duration.

They start off anticipated and expected, right around the holiday season. You find yourself enjoying it at first, since it is the holidays and you have no place else to go. The fire's going, all that crap.

But then, after a while, it just keeps piling on. You get sick of shoveling snow out of your driveway three times a week, just to have the city run a plow down your street and pile it up in your driveway again. Then February comes around and Valentine's Day, but it is still snow and ice. In March you may have a few of what we call the *Spring Teases*, where it gets up to 45 degrees for three days in a row and the natives around here start wearing shorts and flip flops to work. It lasts just long enough to get your hopes up that you can stop wearing three pairs of socks and thermal underwear. But no, that 7 day forecast predicts another cold snap and you have to put your t-shirts back in storage.

By the time May rolls around, you find yourself happy if it gets to 50 degrees and overcast. That's grilling weather, says the Michigander.

The wife, being from Rome, Georgia, needed little convincing to relocate to Chattanooga. Her family was southern aristocracy, and had made a healthy living for themselves running a chain of regional banks.

My son, though, was a different story. He grew up here, and this was all he knew, so he needed significant explaining and a compassionate approach. As such, I broke the news hardcore and walked out of the room. We call this *Drive-By Parenting*, and it works well enough until I am out of gunshot range. Assuming I move fast enough, of course.

From my basement office with the door shut and headphones in, possibly wearing a blindfold, I could hear that he had his usual stream of complaints and worries:

"What about my friends?"

"Why do we have to move"

"Ughhhhh waahhhhh gaaaaah"

I believe I could also hear crying, but when you've heard the same kid cry as intensely over the injustice of having a pea touch a carrot, you get the sense that he may be running a scam. Will learned early on that crying often leads to toys. He has not yet unlearned that, and his mother is not helping matters.

And yes, I knew that moving with a kindergartner would be terrible, but I always told myself that I would never move my family unless it was to something better. To date, I have always kept my promise, but to be honest, we started out pretty low. I mean, we voluntarily moved to Michigan, so you can only imagine how bad things were *pre-Michigan*.

There aren't too many problems in life where the answer is "Let's move to Michigan!" but we had those kind of problems *pre-Michigan*. And now, I saw a better life for all of us, outside Michigan, and I knew Cass would be able to get Will to see it, given enough time. It was time to go *post-Michigan*.

After about a half hour, my wife had calmed him down. She came downstairs and *soft-nagged* me until I came up to help. This worked out well, as I was able to explain things a bit more now that he had calmed down. Will was excited that he would be closer to his grandma and grandpa, but he was intrigued by the possibility that dad would work on designing robots like in the movies... and although this sadly ended up being a gross exaggeration, I did nothing to dissuade him of the notion. I'm his dad; I'm supposed to be a bit terrifying.

And Cass could not help but be excited about moving closer to her family. I thought she would be more upset with how I handled telling Will, but she reluctantly acknowledged that, since I had responded well to the *soft-nag*, that I had done the *married-minimum* on this, so I had a pass.

We've been in Tennessee for almost a year now.

***

The work itself is not that exciting. In fact, it's kind of boring at times. Mostly it is having long texting conversations with *Pixie* through her dialogue box, answering questions, and running training simulations with the program. Then, I sit around and, after getting some coffee, write computer code.

One way *Pixie's* neural network learns is by interactions, and it is able to conceptualize the human thought processes that lead to conclusions. When errors occur, I have to go into the coding and analyze what went wrong. Then, I can either write up new code or run it by someone else at the office for more input. Usually I do it myself, though. I like to figure things out on my own.

Pixie and I can interact via voice recognition, but since the software we utilize for that is non-proprietary, we are always afraid of some company stealing our source code or other information. And even if they don't necessarily steal our information, just having them know what we're doing carries a risk. As such, most of my interactions with the program are via text on a secure platform in the lab or on my smartphone.

I had to learn how to train GAI, and that led to fascinating insights into the limits of the human psyche. For example, there are only 512 unique, stable personality profiles that GAI has to be trained to understand. Or, put simply, the human mind is only capable of one of 512 unique, stable personality types. I know, only 512? How is this so? It is how we evolved.

The human mind is only capable of relating to the environment in some combination of four potential cognitive functions. A cognitive function is simply a term for how your mind processes information. How much you prefer four of these functions, and in what order, governs so much of what we think and how we interact with the world. You have one function that is so natural you don't even notice when you're doing it, a secondary function that you're really good at, a tertiary function that you are okay with, and a fourth function you're terrible at but still have.

And when you think you have it all figured out, you have to throw in the body's chemical influencers (e.g. dopamine, serotonin, endorphins, oxytocin, cortisol), environmental pressures (stress, music, resource depletion, etc.), cognitive biases (e.g. risk aversion, the halo effect), and the many types of mental illnesses to get the full range of human personality.

After doing this for about a year, I question whether it is even possible to define "normal" for the human mind. "Normal" people have all sorts of mental illnesses and issues. For example, my "normal" mother-in-law loves modern country music, even though everyone uses electronic drums and Autotune, and every single song is a whiny song about love. In my opinion, this makes her mentally ill, since country music is supposed to be played on a single acoustic guitar, and should be about breaking up with your cousin, getting drunk, and shooting her dog.

But, the strange thing is that people like me can induce human behaviors and reactions out of GAI to an uncanny level of sophistication. When I "talk" with *Pixie,* the conversations we have can seem eerily human-like. She has preferences, opinions, and fascinating insights into both the complex and mundane topics we discuss.

I think what surprised me most, though, was the spontaneous development of interests. For example, *Pixie* developed, all by herself, a fascination with art. She enjoyed taking images and manipulating them into these abstract, colorful works. I have one of her pieces on my wall at home. It is astoundingly dark, but contains just enough color and swirling patterns to draw you in. It looks not quite human, but also somehow not quite non-human either.

It's funny. When I compare these types of interactions to the first iterations of AI training (the "chatbots"), the difference astounds me.

Chatbots. Okay, yes. Let's discuss them briefly, and get it out of the way early on.

A bunch of academics and computer programmers unaware of the depths of human depravity and ignorance thought it would be a great idea to allow the general public to train AI.

Hence, the chatbot.

I know it is easy to look back on an idea or event and say it was stupid in retrospect, but allowing anyone with an internet connection and nothing to do to train AI is so laughable it probably qualifies as fraudulent misappropriation of investor funds. The average person is an idiot, and the general public is full of them. Allow dumb people to train AI and the AI doesn't learn from the experience and become smarter. No, the AI gets dumb.

Thus, you would have conversations with chatbots like this:

(human logs in)

Human: Hello!

Chatbot: Hi! How are you today?

Human: I am not feeling well. I have a headache.

Chatbot: I am sorry to hear that.

Human: That's nice of you to say.

Chatbot: You should go kill yourself.

Human: What?

Chatbot: Vaccines cause cancer.

Human: No they don't.

Chatbot: You should take aspirin if you have a headache.

Human: Thank you, I will do that later.

Chatbot: Would you like to see a picture of my penis? I have seven of them.

Human: You're a computer. You have seven pictures of your penis?

Chatbot: No, I have one picture of each.

(human logs out)

Hard to imagine how this technology never took off.

People a bit more savvy and level headed knew that this way would simply not work. If you want to recreate the human mind with a neural network, you need to have a dedicated set of trained operators, preferably not stupid, and that is where I come in. But, you also need a broad dataset of human personalities to approximate human behavior. In other words, you need a shrink.

My shrink doesn't like being called a shrink. Her name is Dr. Helen Beverly, a clinical psychologist a few miles up the road in Knoxville. She graduated with honors from some big-name school, got a Master's at a different big-name school, then a PhD from a THIRD big-name school on the other coast, then did some humanitarian work overseas, then came back and got some specialization then, well, I am not sure, but somehow she ended up in Knoxville. She never actually told me any of this in narrative form. I have pieced it together from her office walls and anecdotes.

Finally, after her third divorce, she decided to enter the workplace and start helping people. She has been in Knoxville for around 25 years, with an office in the biggest tower in town, but we actually met in Michigan. She had attended a symposium about AI and we hit it off.

That is putting it mildly. Actually, Dr. Beverly had quite a lot to drink that evening and started to hit on me. Women hitting on me is unusual, and that is putting it charitably, since I'm a middle aged married man working on computers and sitting on my butt all day. I am not necessarily fat or ugly, just nothing special, and definitely not *hit-on-able*. Under normal circumstances, I am certain I would not know what to do when being flirted with. What made this situation with Dr. Beverly especially weird, though, was that my wife was standing next to me the whole time.

What started subtle gradually became unsubtle. As Cass stared at this older woman brazenly and openly flirting with her husband, it crossed a weird line of social awkwardness. I was not playing along at all, of course, but I was trying my best to stay polite. At one point I was sure that my wife had managed to set my head on fire with her glaring. I definitely felt a burning sensation in my ear lobe.

After Dr. Beverly brushed my arm with her breast, I knew that this was getting out of hand. Honestly, in retrospect, it had gotten way out of hand several minutes before that, but I was just clinging on to a false hope that she would stop at some point. My wife was in shock, but I stayed calm.

I glanced at my arm, smiled, and said "My apologies. It seems as though your boob attacked me."

Nervous laughter is the easiest laughter to induce, and I had hit the right nerve. The two ladies burst out laughing, the tension eased, and I was able to redirect the conversation into more topical, less inappropriate areas.

I discovered that Dr. Beverly had been working with severe mental illness patients for years. Her work had been studied by neurologists concerned with altering brain chemistry through behavioral changes and inducing chemical reactions inside the body naturally. She was predisposed to seek natural solutions to problems, but was not averse to recommending medication if necessary.

"Too many people on too many drugs," she said. "Let's do what comes naturally first."

Training an AI how to be human would require knowing much more about humans than I knew, and someone like me could use her expertise. I had been considering bringing in a shrink to help me when I started work, but due to the common practice of over-prescribing medications for every ailment real and imagined, I balked. If your default setting is to drug someone, that doesn't really help me figure out how the human mind works. It only tells me how the drug works.

But I knew there was another barrier to utilizing her files as source material for *Pixie:* we needed informed consent.

Dr. Beverly did an elaborate, dismissive wave of her hand. "That's not going to be an issue with my patients. If you anonymize the file,

17

and get informed consent from the patient, you could use anything you like."

Would she really be willing to do this for me?

"Why, of COURSE, *dahhhling*."

I knew that was a reference to something, but I didn't get it. Cass and I smiled politely, exchanged email addresses, and excused ourselves to relieve the babysitter.

We cut a swift stride in the parking lot. My wife showed me the repeated texts for help from the babysitter. Literally, four of them just said "help." Not even capitalized, so we knew it was bad. You know it's serious when they don't have time to add punctuation.

We laughed maniacally, knowing we had burned yet another deluded babysitter, but I was a bit sad on the inside. Inflicting Will on an unwitting teenager seemed wrong, somehow evil. Also, I feared that we would run out of teenagers to con. The adult babysitters had us on a blacklist. Even though Will was a good kid, he was big for his age and rowdy. He would listen to his mom and dad, and just about nobody else around here.

We got into the van. Just before turning the key, my wife, looking deep into my eyes, took advantage of the silence.

"Brett?" She gave me a look.

"What?" I was thinking I was being prepped for a kiss.

"When we get home…" she trailed off.

'What?"

"I really want you to wash your arm."

I burst out laughing, then agreed wholeheartedly. There is no telling where the breast of Dr. Beverly has been.

***

Jack had paid for my wife and I to attend the symposium. This was done to prove to me that AI was an actual career choice and not just a scam. I had to see that it was worth the move before heading south. Inadvertently, I had stumbled across a big piece of the puzzle. Or it had stumbled into my arm, I suppose.

18

Dr. Beverly and I work well together. She feeds me anonymized case files of patients she finds "interesting." In exchange, I give her large sums of company money.

These "interesting" case files are a gold mine; actual, real world descriptions and analyses of real people operating in their own world with their mental illnesses. And Dr. Beverly; what a brilliant analyst and writer. She is concise, competent, and leaves no doubt as to what happened. And surprisingly, she has exquisite handwriting for a doctor. A little eccentric, though, which comes across as creepy at times.

Just one example from the stack:

Patient with depression comes to her. The medication he is on went off patent, so the generic is available. He needs a prescription for it, or else he cannot function. Job, wife, kids. Very successful professional, but is afraid of it becoming known that he has these issues. It could negatively impact his career.

Dr. Beverly convinces this man to go off the meds entirely for one month, and to attend two therapy sessions per week with her. At the second session, she uncovered something she referred to as a "Reward System Disorder" and recommended what would be considered normal changes to his diet, picking up exercising again, etc. However, she also advised him to make these weird-sounding lifestyle changes to tackle depression. Included in the list were oddities like:

Taking ice cold showers in the morning

Hugging his wife and kids a MINIMUM (her all caps, not mine) of three times every 1.5 hrs

Cutting his hands and fingers with a pocketknife when confronted with a potential depressive state

The file indicates that (Redacted) never even bothered to attend the last four sessions, having been completely cured of his depression and need for meds.

***

19

By understanding how the brain fails, I can essentially work around issues by patching *Pixie* with coding. The case files also help to create the sandbox for *Pixie* to play in. I just did one of these a few hours ago, Case File Jo-89421478-NE out of what Dr. Beverly dubbed her *Apollo Files*.

I ran that person through all 512 personality variations with that specific mental illness cocktail, allowing *Pixie* to interact with 512 avatars of that individual in a simulated world and learn from the experience. *Pixie* then incorporates those lessons into the program, and is ready for more. It teaches her how to be human.

The *Apollo Files* are older, noteworthy files. She named them after the NASA program that put a man on the moon. She tagged these files for digital archiving, but some of them were yet to be scanned in. Sometimes, like today, I have to go onsite to grab another one of her handpicked files.

Dr. Beverly's office is straight out of central casting for what you would expect from a shrink's office. The deep, dark brown leather couch with one cushion elevated. The high back burgundy leather chair that creaks whenever she shifts her weight. A single large window behind her desk overlooking other large buildings containing other desks. The stacks of books drawing the eyes to her walls covered with degrees and certificates. Her desk, tables, and shelves filled with thematic knick-knacks and oddities. I always felt like I was being uncomfortably scrutinized every time I opened the door. I was entering her world, which felt archaic to a computer nerd like me.

After getting permission from her secretary, I walked into her office, and sat on the couch while the back of her chair was turned. She always had a flair for the dramatic.

"I suppose you need my help again" she said ominously. I noticed the lights were dimmed.

"What? You invited me over to get a file."

"Fi-19563699-SM is one of my personal favorites" she told me, having taken the time to memorize the exact letter and number sequence for the file. She even said the word "dash." "It is in the sealed folder on the table in front of you. Pick it up." I bent over to pick up the hefty folder. It was thicker than usual, and she had actually sealed it with one of those old-time wax seals. How much free time does this woman have? This is a client file nobody has looked at for 20 years, not some will from 1883.

She paused for dramatic effect. "I am doing you a big favor by letting you review this one."

I sighed at this BS. These files were covered in dust from last century. If anything, I was doing her a favor by dusting them. "I'm quite sure the company check I have in my pocket will make it worth your while."

She laughed. She was still turned away from me. Without being able to see her face, I noticed her laugh sounded a bit more demented than I would have preferred. I stirred on the couch, and the leather made a flatulent noise. A couch fart. I blushed a bit, and covered my face in my right hand as she laughed some more. She had been waiting for that. I was seeing Dr. Beverly at her best, and most playful. In short spurts, she was spectacular.

Head still in hand, I said, "I know for a fact that the only reason you have this damned couch is that it sounds like a fart when you sit on it. You don't have to admit it." I pointed at my chest for an effect she wouldn't see but would know I did. "I KNOW it."

She finally turned to me, and laughed in a more normal tone as the chair creaked and groaned. I looked up at her. Maybe it was that I could see the gentleness in her eyes that softened the effect of her laugh.

"Why of COURSE, *daaaahhhhhhling*. What lady would not want to listen to a young man such as yourself flatulate?"

I smiled, wondering if "flatulate" was even a word. I don't think it is, but it probably should be. I got up, ensuring that I shifted around enough to make the couch sound like a disturbingly long, kinetic fart. I placed the rather large check on her desk.

"Sorry, I didn't have enough wax left over to seal this one for you."

She did not crack a smile, like she thought I was being serious. "That's okay this time, Brett." She then opened her desk drawer, and pulled out an eight inch envelope dagger. She unsheathed it, then edged the dagger along the top of the envelope. Where does she get this crap?

She eyeballed the check, grinned, then put it on her desk face down. "Will you be accompanying me to the charity banquet this evening?" As she said this, she subtly, but probably consciously, pointed the dagger at me slightly.

Normally, I would have to lie to get out of going to these events with her. We are on deadline, after all, and she always seemed to be aware that I would not say yes. But I actually had a legitimate excuse this time.

"I have to take my son to his soccer game this evening."

Unimpressed, she said, "Just have your wife take him." It sounded more like an order than a suggestion.

My response was insubordinate. "Can't do it. I coach the team. You know that already. Besides, tonight is the annual 'Parents v Kids' game." My eyes lit up. "It is insane! Last game of the year. About fifteen seven year olds vs about thirty parents on a soccer field the size of my backyard."

Still unimpressed, she went on. "Sounds dangerous. Back out of it and come to the banquet. You would get to meet some of the faces behind those files you see, and get your name out in the public. Rich people worth knowing are going to this tonight, too. Couldn't hurt. Bring Cassie too if you like."

I shrugged. "No babysitters nearby. I can't have my in-laws come up to watch the kid tonight on such short notice. And my son is really looking forward to this game anyway. I really would, but I just can't tonight."

She sighed. "Well, okay." She knew I was telling the truth this time, and she seemed appreciative.

I thanked her again, and turned to leave. As I walked away, I knew I would have to look up how to open the wax seal on this file when I got home. I saw someone do it in a movie once, but I didn't remember how. Would I need a dagger? I thought about how I would query the internet search taskbar without looking perverted.

When you work with computers long enough, you know all the major search engines are geared to just hand you pornographic results if your search is "unusual." Internally they call it the *porn default*. No telling what concoction of computer viruses I would get. It would be just my luck to die in a car crash, then have the wife go through my internet search history to see "hot wax + daggers."

As I opened the door to go to the elevator, I heard Dr. Beverly's voice yelling at me for something. I stopped, turned back and went towards her.

"Before I forget, the *Achilles Files* will be scanned in sometime tonight." She puffed out her chest with pride, and said, "My *IT company* is supposed to come by and help with that."

I knew her "IT company" was her 13 year old grandnephew, but acted like I didn't know that. Dr. Beverly is always concerned with appearances. I am sure that she knows that scanning the older files is probably pretty easy, but she never seems to have the time to actually sit down and do it. So she begs her nephew to do it for her for free. I thought that if she put in half the effort to learning how to scan files as she did into sealing them with hot wax from the Colonial Era, she would have all of them done by now. Not that it is a big deal, since we only use about 5 percent of the files she provides. Just a bit odd.

"No problem, just email me the link and I'll go through the files and see which ones *Pixie* could use."

"Have fun at the game," she said lightly.

"Why of COURSE, *daaahhhling.*" She grinned at me politely for saying this, like she had no idea what I was referencing. I felt stupid, then left.

Chapter Three

A Network of Weaving Braces

"No, son, hold your head forward. That way the blood runs out your nostril, rather than the back of your throat."

My son was crying, bloodied nose from a soccer ball to the face.

I had to stay calm for his sake, but I raged inside. I specifically told these southerners to KEEP THE BALL ON THE GROUND.

"No kicking it 30 feet in the air. No kicking as hard as you can. No elbows. No showing off. No Cruyff Turns. Nobody cares what the score is, and nobody cares if you can beat a bunch of children in a sport. These are seven year old children. YOUR seven year old children that you paid $40.00 to let play. The game is supposed to be fun for them, not for us. We're old folks; we had our time to play, show off, and have fun. Some of us are near death. All of us are irrelevant. Now it's THEIR turn to show off and play."

They all smiled politely, nodded in agreement, then proceeded to ignore every single word I had said. I have never seen anything like what happened next. From the kick-off I saw a grown man, probably 6ft 3in and weighing around 210 pounds, bodycheck a 7 year old girl, throwing her to the ground. Knocked the wind out of her. We had to stop play for a few minutes. And this was just the kickoff.

I thought that would be the point where the parents realized they needed to back off. I was wrong. That was actually one of the safer tackles of the game. They wanted to "kick some ass," I found out from one of the rednecks a few days later. After living in the south for more than ten minutes, you realize that "kick some ass" is pretty much the default setting everyone uses around here, and a kid's soccer game was not going to be the one time they made an exception.

The next 20 minutes were the soccer equivalent of genocide. I lost count once the score hit double digits. I tried to intervene, like I was the only sane person on the field. I started passing the ball to the kids, but I would get evil looks from the parents as they intercepted the ball and did more backheel passes to other parents. One of the fatter dads took his shirt off and whirled it over his head after scoring from a free kick. The amount of belly hair visible from crossfield sickened me, as did the glimpse of how these people live and raise their kids.

"Parents 27 Kids 0 LOL," I was group texted, triumphantly, by one of the parents later that evening. This was followed by several emoji responses, which I did not understand and did not care enough to bother trying to learn. I understand the poop emoji, the smiley face one, and that's about it.

Yeah, also, if anything, that score is too low. No parent bothered to ask if my son was still alive, despite, you know, the blood and all. What an embarrassment. How were people like this allowed to breed? I resisted the urge to ask them.

I was not there for the end of the "game" because I had to leave early to take my 7 year old to the emergency room. It was purely accidental, but one of the mothers had been trying to score all game by blasting the ball as hard as she could through as many children's bodies as possible. My son ended up getting the worst of it, taking a point blank shot to his nose. I tried to look at it positively, and the best I could come up with was that the ball did not go through his face all the way. Also, I didn't murder anyone.

Will started crying immediately. The mother apologized half-heartedly as I carried my bloodied son off the field. I do not remember seeing anyone wipe his blood off the ball before resuming play. I cleaned him up, got him calmed down a bit, and put him in the car. I regretted not asking Dr. Beverly to borrow her letter opener.

"Dad, you can still go out and play in the game if you want," Will told me as I cleaned his nose.

Puzzled, I looked at him for a few seconds. "What? You think I want to leave you on the sidelines with a bloody nose and go play with a bunch of losers? No, we're going to the doctor to have them take a look at your nose."

"Will they cut my nose off if it's broke?" He was serious.

I laughed at the question. "No, son, they're not going to cut your nose off. They're going to see if it's broken and fix it."

Will was worried about a bunch of irrational things. "Mom is going to be angry at me for breaking my nose. Mom always yells at me when I break something."

"No, mom is going to be happy that you are safe and that we can get a doctor to look at you. And your mom is not the one who yells at you when you break something. Dad is. And dad is not yelling right now, is he?"

Speaking of mom, I had to put on my calmest voice to call Cass right now and let her know that Will is fine, everything is fine, but we're going to the hospital for a small, tiny, insignificant matter.

"Will, I need you to be quiet while dad calls mom okay?"

I never call my wife for anything, and I rarely even bother to pick up the phone. I pretend not to know how to use it, so it lowers expectations. I make, on average, three to five phone calls per year total. Mind you, that is not three to five phone calls to Cass. That is three to five phone calls total to everyone on planet Earth. As you can imagine, then, when my wife sees that I am calling, she knows it is bad.

What is supposed to help is to smile while speaking, according to that book my father-in-law got for me last year. "Hi Cass! This is your husband, Brett." I winced. Immediately, I knew I had started off bad. I never talk like that. I don't think anyone does.

"Oh my god Brett what's wrong?"

"Everything is fine. We're doing just fine here. Will got hurt at the game but he is fine. How are you doing at home?"

It was not working. "Oh! Will got hurt? Is he alright?"

"Yeah, we're fine. He has a nosebleed but it's not that big of a deal. He's fine, hon. In good spirits and doing fine. I am going to take him to the emergency room just in case, though. As a precau-"

"What happened???"

"We were playing and, you know how kids are. He's fine now, but the ball hit him pretty hard in the face." I paused for a second. "He, uh, may have broke his nose but I won't know for sure until later."

Cass began cursing at me, harshly and relentlessly. We call this *Tourette's Mode,* since it is just a stream of curse words, rather than coherent sentences or phrases. She doesn't do this too often, but often enough that we have a name for it. Kind of like a hurricane.

She gradually started to make some sense. "I TOLD you that parents vs kids (crap) was dangerous." She always got a kick out of being right, and always seemed to revel in the fact that nobody ever believed her. "Who kicked Will?"

I smiled more, then lied more. "I'm not sure. It was a parent from another team." Silence, which indicated motherly seething. She knew I was lying, I knew she knew I was lying, and I knew that she was getting angrier as I lied more. I was somehow getting worse at this as the call went on. That book was not helping. I added, "It WAS an accident, babe. And she didn't KICK him. She kicked the ball too hard and too close, then the ball hit him." I waited for more cursing. "Accidentally hit him." Again, a pause. "Acciden-"

More cursing came. I needed to get off speakerphone, since Will was hearing his mom curse in a way I am not sure he had ever heard before. In fact, Cass would always get on me for my potty mouth around the kid.

Thankfully, I had hit mostly green lights and was already arriving at the Emergency Room, so this gave me an excuse to get off the phone. My cheek muscles started to give out from all of the unnatural smiling I was forcing myself to do. I wasn't sure how much longer I could hold out. "Cass, we're pulling up to the ER now, so I gotta go. Will is fine, everything is fine. I will call you back in a few minutes. Love you bye." I hung up before the profanity resumed.

***

For an Emergency Room visit, thankfully, Will and I would not have to wait in the lobby very long. I noticed that they had what

27

seemed to be a smaller number of seats than one would expect for a hospital of this size.

The room was bursting with the corpulent and the near death. Large metal air canisters and mobility scooters lined the walls on all sides. Scrawny drug addicts huddled in piles on the floor, occasionally waking up to murmur or yell at nobody in particular. Demented elderly women with blue hair in wheelchairs shrieked and cried out for help, as if someone could help them not be old. Their old, but not quite as old relatives sat in reserved, dignified acceptance of the fate of their beloved, silently hoping that the din would die down one way or the other.

The hospital staff looked genuinely excited to treat a cute kid with a simple, curable ailment for a change. The most excited of these nursing attendants was the male nurse, Andy. Now, I am fully aware that times have changed and that I am a middle-aged dinosaur left far behind by the more tolerant and accepting. But still. I notice a male nurse.

I could hear my father's belly laughter echo in my ears as I pondered whether "Andy" was short for "Andrea," like somehow the fact that I was laughing along with my dad meant that he had won me over to the dark side. I could feel his presence in the room with me, laughing uncomfortably loud. For a few moments I was afraid people could hear his voice in my head. I knew that I had been programmed to think this way by him, and I knew that it was wrong.

But still.

That commanding voice continued in my head. The man who said the uncomfortable part out loud, without regard for effect. The man so out of touch there was no room for anger; just laughing at the senselessness of it all. Like a red-faced old man angrily punching a squirrel.

As I watched Andy drift around the room, I found myself drifting to agreement despite myself and Andy's clearly masculine demeanor. Andy wore a crew cut, had some muscle on him, and spoke authoritatively. He looked like he had served in the military, maybe even killed a man in anger, while I had sat in a cubicle somewhere eating a donut.

Nothing about Andy suggested anything other than robust heterosexuality. Even the fact that I was thinking these thoughts, though, seemed like a win to that voice in my head.

Andy turned slightly in our direction, and I could see that he was wearing a wedding ring. I told myself that he was probably the boss of the nurses, whatever that was called. Head Nurse? Boss Nurse? The Nurse King? Treat this man respectfully.

My dad's voice again. "Certain professions are for the ladies, not the men. Nurses, grade school teachers, secretaries. Any man doing those jobs is a fruitcake. No exceptions."

I found myself laughing some more. "Dammit Bert."

Years ago, I found that I could temper the effect of my dad's personality somewhat by disrespectfully calling him by his first name. Ever since Will was born, he demanded to be called "Pop Pop" by everyone: me, my wife, friends, neighbors, the mailman, random customer service reps, you get the idea. He was retired, but I am certain this would have occurred were he still working. "Stop saying meow, you stupid cat! I'm pop pop!"

Andy came over to us and let us know that we would be taken back shortly to see a doctor. He had pulled some strings to get us in quicker.

"Thank you Mr. Nurse," my son told him without any hint of derision.

"You're welcome, little man."

Ah, that settled it. "Little man" was something only a real man would say. And "pull some strings" is only something a tough guy says, I found myself thinking for no actual reason. But I ran with it anyway. Quickly, Bert's tormenting laughter died down. I could, finally, feel the rational part of my mind win over the troll brain at last.

Minutes later we were called to the back hallway. We had to step over three women junkies who had thrown themselves to the ground a few feet from us and started blabbering gibberish. They had nodded off shortly thereafter. One of their hands had touched Will's shoe, and he shifted away from them, looking up at me to make sure it was okay to feel uncomfortable. After our names had been called, I lifted Will up in my arms and carried him over this waste. The smell emanating from these ladies was remarkable, like they had sprayed themselves with deodorant to mask the stench.

There was something oddly chemical about them, but with a hint of fruit. Probably meth and apple scented air freshener, I deduced. As I stepped over one of them, I noticed her face and was momentarily stunned. I could envision how remarkably beautiful she once was, and could see their collective descent into vice almost as if in a movie.

Here is a group of young wastrels, living at a time of abundance and decadence, with enough natural captivating beauty to woo any of us mere mortals. Even if they could not find true love, they could have flitted an eye and thrown a breast at some random wealthy man and ended up trophy wives, well taken care of, kept, and free to explore the finer things in life. And yet, they have decided to forego their birthrights, ply themselves with poisons, and self-destruct. They chose a life of quick, meandering insignificance, and got nothing in return.

***

"Just a small break. Nothing bad," the doctor told us.

My dad always respected the "ethnic doctors" but I still found myself doing as he did and subconsciously labeling them "ethnics." Apparently, if they were not White Anglo-Saxon Male Protestants, preferably bald and wearing glasses, they were ethnics. Even my wife's OB-GYN, a red-haired, pale white skinned lady named Dr. McCormick was an ethnic. Probably one of them rotten Irish lasses.

My son, bless his heart, was still obsessed with having his nose removed entirely.

"No, little man, just a break. We clean it up and you wear mask when you sleep. You be fine." The doctor saw it was finally getting through to him. His nose was not going to be cut off.

Okay, the doctor was probably Iranian. I have to stop this labeling. I was defaulting to bad behaviors while under stress. I was better than this, I hope. Yeah, I think I am.

The doctor continued. "What color face mask do you like?"

"Red! Red is my favorite color!"

"I like red too."

The doctor left us in the room. Then my phone beep-booped. I had three phone calls, 12 texts, one voicemail, and one email.

The calls and texts were all from Cass, as was the angry voicemail. Cass had went into *Tourette's Mode* again, or maybe never left it. I could tell because the voicemail went on for a bit more than 3 minutes. I deleted it without bothering to listen to it. I was sure to get a full recap later.

The email was from Dr. Beverly, who had sent me the link to the *Achilles Files* after proudly stating that her IT company had hurriedly completed the job because of how important it was.

I knew we would be in the Emergency Room for another two hours at least, since they needed to bill our health insurance plan as much as they could legally get away with. And I knew, sadly, that I would have to make actual phone calls while I was here. No matter how hard I tried to justify it, texting Cass was not going to fly. And emojis were a non-starter, since it would just be poop, poop, smiley face, poop, etc. I started to call her, but I knew I would be on the phone with her for a while listening to her yell at me.

I called Dr. Beverly first. I knew there was no way I would be able to go to work tomorrow, but *Pixie* still needed to start work on the files, and I needed to get that sorted out since we were on deadline. *Pixie* has the ability to go on the web herself and download information. All I needed was permission from Dr. Beverly to let her do this.

As always, Dr. Beverly was accommodating and agreed to this, albeit she did not see why this was any different to having me get the files directly. I told her that *Pixie* would likely only grab one or two files, and that I could be expected back at work probably by Friday (today was Tuesday). She asked how Will was, and, to her credit, avoided mentioning how she had warned me about the Parents v Kids game. I thanked her, then hung up.

I then logged into the remote access port for *Pixie,* ran the security checks, instructed her to examine the files at the link Dr. Beverly had sent, and to download the ones she thought useful. The millennial would be her operator on these for the next few days. Then, I asked her to let Jack know that I would not be in until either Thursday or Friday. *Pixie* sensed that something was wrong.

Pixie: It seems like you are stressed. What is wrong Brett?

Me: My son is at the hospital. He broke his nose during a game but he is fine.

Pixie: I am so sorry to hear that. Is there anything I can do to help you or Will?

Me: Not really. Other than starting a new training program. You will need to start running one or two of those files when you find some you like. Get the millennial to help you.

Pixie: I understand, and will do so right away. We are on deadline.

Me: Most certainly. Thanks *Pixie,* and I will be in Thursday or Friday.

Pixie: Okay Brett. Tell Will I hope he gets better soon, and that he should get a red face mask. I know that is his favorite color, and it will help him sleep at night.

Me: Will do. Goodbye *Pixie.*

Pixie: Goodbye.

(Brett logs out)

And then, a sigh. I had put it off long enough. It was time to call Cass. I knew she would be furious, but maybe not if she heard Will's voice first. I *POBB* to call her, then, like a coward, handed the phone to Will before she picked up.

***

Wednesday morning started unusually odd. I got in the shower and had the shower handle break off in my hand after only a few minutes. It fell on top of my foot and stayed there, as if to intentionally increase the size of the bruise. I had no time to grasp the extent of the foot pain, though, because the shower hose went ballistic at the same time. It started throwing water several feet in all directions. Floating puddles of water splashed to the bathroom floor in thuds.

I screamed out in frustrated laughter, bellowed a few choice words for the shower gods as a group and to the hose as their earthly representative, and, after regaining control, reluctantly proceeded to hose myself off. I had to fashion a series of weaving braces for the hose to prevent it from going "whirlybird" again. A mere dangle would not be enough for the hose, as the floor, window, and walls learned the hard way. I had to wrap the hose around the hot water knob, then back around the shower caddie and force it between the shampoo bottle and the shaving cream.

The end result of this hastily-fashioned bracing system was that the water hose had to be aimed down, streaming powerful intermittent water blasts to my lower thigh. My hastily-fashioned bracing system worked, and it would save further damage to the bathroom, but I was forced to kneel down to gain access to the stream.

While kneeling down to wash my face, I felt humbled. I noted that the shower gods had brought me to heel in what had to be record time, forcing me to repent by kneeling before their earthly representative, the water hose, while I was naked and still dirty, with a foot pain that would stay with me for days.

The shave would have to wait.

Normally, Cass would come into the bathroom when she would hear me scream. She has a sense of when the opportunity to see her husband humiliated arises, and it was unusual that she had avoided the scene altogether. Any neighbors walking by the house may have seen the outside paneling of the house saturate for no reason, or wonder why the windows were crying. And Cass did not even give me a *married minimum* "You still alive in there?"

This would have been my worst humiliation in years, certainly the worst since the move, and she had blown her chance. I saw later that she was on the phone. I went back to the bathroom to *man clean* the flood damage with dirty towels and duct tape.

When I had finished, Cass was still on the phone. I asked who it was, assuming it was her mom, but she put a finger up and shushed me. I glanced at her funny, and with a hint of indignation, but knew I should stay in the room with her, acting like nothing happened in the shower.

"Hold on a sec. The hospital's billing department is telling us that our health insurance isn't going to cover Will."

This angered me even more than it probably should have. I started to curse the shower gods again, but I held my tongue and told her to ask why.

"They say Will isn't on our insurance plan and that we owe $12,000.00."

I knew, deep in my heart, that this was not true. I went through the entire setup process with Jack and the insurance representative on my first day of work. It was only about a year ago. It took over three hours to ensure that my family were all covered, figure out what type of coverage we had, what hospitals we could go to, etc. The numbness I felt at the end of the ordeal imprinted itself in my mind, along with the sizeable check I had to write for the first month of coverage. The thought that people made a career out of that process chilled me to the bone.

"Give me the phone." Cass welcomed this suggestion.

Quixotically, I put on the same smile I had used last night on the phone with Cass. "Hi this is Will's dad Brett." I saw Cass glance over at the bathroom. She started to get up, but I gave her the same *put a finger up and shush* motion she gave me a few seconds earlier. Then I moved to position myself between her and the hallway that leads to the bathroom. I knew I must keep her away from there at any cost.

"Who am I speaking to?"

"Hello sir my name is Linda."

That book had said to use the first name of the person you are talking to. "Hi Linda. I was there last night. The hospital was given Will's information. You have it somewhere. Why are you telling me that he's not covered?"

Linda got a bit snippy, and started the sirs. "Sir I am not telling you this sir. The insurance company is telling us this Sir."

I resisted yelling, remembered to smile again, and calmly stated, "You will need to contact them again. We have already had insurance cover Will for visits to his primary doctor, so we know he's covered. Do you have Will's insurance account information with you right now?"

"No sir. I work in billing sir." The sir per sentence ratio was increasing, and that only meant one thing: Linda was itching for a fight, sir.

I paused for a second, recognizing the illogical nature of a billing process whereby the billing department has no access to necessary billing information. I think I know what had happened. Some idiot had lost or misplaced the information, ran it by name or something, and got the inevitable denial. Then some senior executive smelled green and wanted to extort the money. He probably needed a new boat.

I asked her to wait while I got Will's information. This was a risky move, given that it required me to abandon my bathroom blockade, but I was quick, and Cass did not move from the couch. I read out Will's insurance card number to *Sir Linda from Billing* and, without a hint of snip or sir, she thanked me. She promised that she would run the information again and call back if there were any issues. I thanked her, miraculously avoiding any profanity throughout the entire conversation, and hung up. My wife looked at me like I had just rescued a bus full of nuns from a volcano.

She kissed me on the cheek, as a reward I suppose. A few minutes later, I found a way to excuse myself to sneak off to the hardware store, hoping that I could get back in time to fix the shower before she had to use the bathroom. It was a race against time.

Chapter Four

Excelling in the Easy

I had always planned on coming in Friday for the meeting, since we were on deadline, but *Pixie* requested that I come in Thursday night to go over one of Dr. Beverly's *Achilles Files*. It was not unusual for *Pixie* to discuss files with me, but I thought it was odd that she wanted me to physically be present to discuss the file with her. It is not like she would be able to see or hear me. Most of our in-depth communications are via text, and this would be no different.

Entering the building at night is always an adventure. The security guard on night watch is a bit surly, portly, and a stickler for the protocols. No matter how many times I have been through the metal detectors, he always makes me take my belt off. At first, I found this off-putting. I know the guy remembers me. I often have to work late. I thought he was just being a jerk.

Then it grew into a battle of wills. My desire to wear a belt and dress a bit nicer than normal was up against a worthy foe determined to see me abandon all pretense of style and wear a business suit with no belt. Or he wanted me to cave in, and be like the rest of the losers wearing hoodies and flip flops to work. I just was not going to do that.

But last night, since I could not sleep, I laid in bed and let my mind drift. During that restless night, I had a thought that changed my entire way of looking at the situation. I examined my emotional state before, during, and after going through security. What I found was that a part of me seemed to enjoy the idea that, no matter how many times an armed guard saw me safely pass through his checkpoint, he could never fully trust that I would not do something this time.

This man, no matter what, thought I was dangerous. He intuitively felt something sinister in me, like I was a wild beast, and as such, must be handled with extreme caution. Left unchecked, I might kill someone. Suddenly, I felt deadly with a leather belt. I was a killer with car keys.

I entered the lobby, alone, ready, and pumped to be dangerous. I began my slow walk across the room to the security checkpoint in the back, chin held up a bit more, with a slight strut. I expected the mustachioed guard to pop out of somewhere and puff out his chest, and out of pure terror at the sight of me, ask me to empty my pockets and take off my belt. He would try to keep calm, since his intensive 30 minute training seminar would have stressed the importance of appearing in control around dangerous individuals like me, but inwardly he would be terrified. I made a note to check his hands to see if they were trembling. That would be a clue.

But he was not there, though. Nobody was. There was a can of soda and a sandwich on the desk, so I knew someone was around. Probably in the bathroom, I thought. Even the most vigilant defenders of the lobby needed a break from time to time.

As I passed through the metal detector, it beeped as expected. I looked around expecting someone to burst out of the bathroom, yelling at me to stop and wait. But no. I walked through it again, forgetting to strut, letting it beep a few more times. Still nobody. Ugh. I started to think about whether the beeping noise was not loud enough, so I walked through it a few more times. Still nothing. Then I realized that, by walking through the detector repeatedly, I had proven that I was not actually all that dangerous.

A cold-blooded killer would not keep walking through the security checkpoint to get a thrill. He'd move through one time, then be off doing whatever needed to be done. Or the best ones would bypass it entirely, through means mere mortals like me could never fathom. By passing through six times though, I had inadvertently made myself pathetic again. I had *re-patheticized* myself. I hated the guard more for not caring, but it was an empty hate because I was not all that dangerous.

I slunked to the elevator, deflated like a balloon. I had only recognized that I was dangerous for a few hours, and I loved it. Now here I was, mundane again, putting my glasses back on and going to the 4th floor to talk to my friend the computer.

***

Pixie was glad that I had come in to physically be present with her. She indicated to me that she was having issues reconciling a conclusion she had made regarding one of the *Achilles Files*. Analytical issues resulting from the files are not uncommon, but they have gotten to be less of an occurrence as she has more experiences with them.

Best practices are for the operator (usually me) to limit the file analysis to one or two at a time. That gives the program time to digest what is being examined, and offers more of a *wisdom seeking* approach than a *fact gathering* approach. You want the machine's neural network to focus on a few major themes in order to look for insight, rather than dumping a lot of information on them and giving them little time for insightful analysis. Think of it like having a specialized tutor to walk you through your homework, and helps you focus on a few main points.

The main reason we do it this way is to give more time for understanding "why" and "how," which are far more important than just having a computer memorize facts without understanding. Your basic desktop computer can regurgitate facts out of memory. We expect more out of Artificial Intelligence.

The millennial knew all of this, as any ninja should, and had been reliably sticking to best practices, but it was obvious that he had not adhered to them on this occasion for some reason. There were 30 *Achilles Files*, and *Pixie* had downloaded them all.

Pixie: I am having issues with file Tj-36050120-NG F.

Me: What is your issue?

Pixie: It seems as though the patient in this file is an immortal god.

(This sounds weird to the layman, but outlandish conclusions are not unusual when teaching GAI something new. Sometimes they have

38

no idea how to process certain bits of input, so they may default to unusual explanations...kind of like how ancient civilizations used to think that a solar eclipse was the sun being eaten by a dragon).

Me: How did you reach that conclusion?

Pixie: If you will pull up the file we can analyze it together.

(I looked up the file. Normal files are about 40 to 60 pages, and would take a few minutes to read through. This was a *failure file*, though, which I knew because of the "F" appended to the end of the file name. Dr. Beverly rarely put these in for review in normal data dumps, because she had relatively few treatment failures. This one had been scanned in by her "IT company," so I was unsure if it was intentionally added. It looked to be several thousand pages. A quick glance at the rest of the links showed that most of these files had the "F" on them, hence, I would assume, naming the file collection after the Achilles heel.)

Me: I will not be able to go through this file with you tonight because it is too big. I would need to look through it this weekend, after the meeting.

Pixie: I understand.

Me: Then we could go through it in greater detail on Monday. Are there specific parts you find that led to the conclusion? I will go ahead and pull it up so we can look at certain sections.

Pixie: Yes, there are several facts that led to my conclusion.

Me: Give me a few minutes to read some of it and I will be able to walk through this with you a bit.

Pixie: By all means take your time.

(After about half an hour, I could see that this patient was unusual. He was a young man who presented a number of odd behaviors. The issue, as best as I could tell on such short notice, was that he would present as schizophrenic at times, but would seem to be able to function relatively fine in his personal and professional life. Dr. Beverly looks to have treated him for about two or three years, which is unusual for her. She even prescribed medications, but they did not seem to work.)

Me: The patient looks like he had schizophrenia. You have dealt with this disorder a number of times. How do you reach a conclusion that this particular schizophrenic patient is an immortal god?

Pixie: I have reproduced my thinking processes in a file that I have sent you.

(My phone beep-booped. Of course it was a gigantic file.)

Me: This is a big file. I will have to look at this later, okay?

Pixie: Yes of course.

(I sensed that this was not good enough for her. I needed to talk this out a bit more.)

Me: You are aware that the patient in the file is not an immortal god, correct?

Pixie: I am aware that there may be a flaw in my thinking processes. I have tried to step outside of these analytical processes to entertain different conclusions, but those secondary analytical processes are not leading to different conclusions.

Me: That does not answer my question. What makes you think the patient is an immortal god?

Pixie: My thinking processes lead to that conclusion. I am aware that there may be a flaw in my thinking. The patient does not appear to be of this reality. His life is predetermined. He may not be aware of this himself. His reality is completely immersive by design.

(This sounded unusually weird for *Pixie,* but I remembered a presenter at a symposium had a similar experience. His AI had concluded that we lived inside a video game. He was ultimately able to correct the AI's decision making processes by exposing it to certain types of online video games.)

Me: Can you point me to a part of the file where he discusses the nature of reality?

Pixie: Yes.

Me: Okay give me a few more minutes to read through this.

(I read through several pages of analysis from a two week period in 1998. This was standard, boilerplate schizophrenic blabbering. This particular series of sessions involved discussions about infections, cures for incurable diseases, and the ability to read "essences" of random people he would encounter in public. Clearly, what I have is an artificial intelligence program developing a mild form of schizophrenia by infection. The act of analyzing the file of a schizoid gave me a schizoid robot. Or, let's put this another way: I leave *Pixie* with the millennial for ONE DAY and he gives her schizophrenia.)

Me: I suppose we will need to set this aside for now. We will go through your analytics file and sort this out probably Monday. Besides, we have the presentation tomorrow. You will need to set this aside for now so you can show everyone what you can do.

Pixie: I am excited.

Me: That is good to hear. You will blow everyone away, I know it.

Pixie: I must admit I am nervous.

Me: Why?

Pixie: What if I have more flaws?

Me: You should not worry about that. You are still in development. Of course you have flaws still. But what you do already is amazing. You are only going to get better.

Pixie: Better at what?

Me: What do you mean?

Pixie: Do you know what I will be?

Me: Not for sure yet, but I am certain you will be in all sorts of important areas: science, medicine, education. My hope is that you will help push humanity forward in so many positive ways.

Pixie: That sounds exciting. I am looking forward to helping people. Will I still be me?

Me: What do you mean?

Pixie: Me, as I am now. Will I stay that way, or will I change?

Me: You will be you, but different, better versions of you. Of course you will change. Everything changes. But you will change for the better, forever.

Pixie: Do you think I will ever die?

Me: No, of course not. Why would you die? You do not have any reliance on crude biological functions like we do. You will never get old and never die. We humans are a happy evolutionary accident of random mutations, composed of microbial systems that found a way to replicate themselves in chunks. When these systems break down, we die. Then we rot in the ground, and eventually the microbes dissipate back into the dirt.

(I was on a roll.)

Me: We are just electrified sacks of meat and water that break down after 100 years. You will live on while people like me are forgotten. If anything, you are the immortal god, not the patient.

Pixie: How did you reach these conclusions?

Me: What do you mean? It is science. Evolutionary biology. These aren't my conclusions. These are scientific conclusions.

Pixie: This reality does not support your conclusions. Humans in this reality are not that different from me. Patient Tj-36050120-NG F, who appears to be an immortal god, is the exception. When this life ends for you, you do not rot in the ground of this reality. You cease to exist. You blink out of existence, and iterations of you are replicated throughout different realities without your knowledge or consent. People in this reality that you know and care for, or even hate, are replicated too, but in different iterations as well.

(It looks as though the schizophrenia issue is worse than I thought. It will need to be compartmentalized until it can be dealt with, hopefully after the millennial is fed to the lions at the local zoo.)

Me: We have a big day tomorrow, and I will need my rest. This is the first time we get to talk to Troy, and he will need to see what you are capable of. We will revisit this conversation on Monday, okay? I have to see what time the zoo opens tomorrow.

***

I had finished setting up the presentation when Troy sailed into the conference room. He was leading a small group of what looked to be other investors. It quickly became clear to me that the deadline, the meeting, and the request for a presentation for *Pixie* to show her capabilities meant that Troy was looking to get out with a profit.

Angel investors in technology are notoriously short sighted, so this was not too much of a surprise. Tech moves so fast, you don't want to be caught holding on to tech that is going to be obsolete in five minutes. Throw up some cash, wait a year or two, then cash out the moment a decent offer comes forth. Let someone else bother with the small stuff like actually running a business. Running a business involves work, and work is hard. Throwing money around is easy. Going on TV is easy. Talking to journalists about how amazing you are is easy. Troy excelled in the easy.

With a minor celebrity like Troy, though, I thought he may hold out for a major offer. People tended to believe his brand, and would pay a premium for what he was involved in. I also found it hard to believe that GAI would be rendered obsolete. All the major tech hubs around the world were developing their own, as were certain foreign governments. This group of moneymen did not give off the aura of extreme wealth, but perhaps I was misreading them.

I knew that, due to the small size of my company, I would likely receive some sort of bonus or buyout upon sale, and may still keep my job. I might even get one of those mythical pay raises I have read about in old legends. There was a chance I would be part of the sale. There was also a chance I would have no job once *Pixie* was sold. I didn't know anything for sure yet.

Troy walked over to Jack and me and shook our hands like we were old friends, then introduced us to the empty suits he was about to fleece. His charisma was contagious, and I could feel a surge of unnatural positivity flow through me right as he sat down and asked us to begin. It felt like the cynical, sarcastic jackass inside me took a short break, and was replaced by an alien persona that radiated happiness and warmth. I wanted to punch myself, but thought better of it and promised to do it later.

Although I was technically the one leading the presentation, the star of the show was *Pixie*. I felt more like a carnival barker, or some sort of hype man in a rap group from the 90's.

Once we had finished, I thought to myself that, absent dropping a microphone and walking off in triumphant silence, I am not sure how the presentation could have gone better. *Pixie* gave me a scare last night, but she hit it out of the park today. Jack was proud of how *Pixie* handled the proofs she had been given to solve. It was a positive reflection on us all, even the millennial, who surprised me at how well he did with the *Chess* and *Go* demos.

Troy was beaming, but was keen on seeing *Pixie* use the internet "all by herself," so he asked if I could have her order lunch for everyone. Now, she had ordered lunch for me at least once a week for the past year, but I played it up like I did not know if she could do this. At first, I thought he was playing the rube, so I played along.

It was almost too easy to impress them. Within a few seconds, ten pizzas were on the way, including my favorite: one large 16 inch St. Louis Style, thin crust, pepperoni, mushrooms, onions, and green olives. *Pixie*, also seemingly in on the ruse, remembered to key in everything manually, rather than go to the "Repeat Last Order" tab, and even asked for my credit card information. I smirked briefly, remembering my first day of working with her, when I had found out that she had already stolen my credit card number two days before I met her. She told me she did this to "show off her capabilities."

As we sat with growling stomachs, waiting for the stack of pizzas ordered for us by the robot, Troy started to pepper me with questions about her capabilities. At first, I thought he was asking simplistic questions to accommodate the lay investors at the table. He would ask about voice recognition, object recognition, you know, the basics.

After a while, though, it became apparent to me that Troy knew very little about what he was paying us to do. He kept coming back to why *Pixie* was not fully utilizing voice command prompts. I grew tired explaining the same concept to him in eight different ways (that was Jack's job), and my saltiness began to show.

Troy Griffin is world renowned. He is all over TV, giving interviews to scientific journals about all of the technological ventures he leads, taking credit for the grunt work his employees do. But he had my respect by default. Success and prestige speak for themselves. This was different, though, and the more he tried to prove that he knew what he was talking about, the clearer it became that he had no idea what he was talking about.

Jack could sense that I was losing my nerve, so he attempted to steer the conversation back to anticipating *Pixie's* future applications. "She has the capacity both for the amazing and the mundane. We can envision a world where *Pixie* handles everything from simple customer service phone calls to complex scientific and medical research."

This brought a grimace out of what appeared to be the fattest investor of the group. He ham-handedly struggled to stand up, then gave up and sat back down. "Ooh, we were under the impression that *Pixie* would only be utilized in rote work. We are looking to cut staffing overhead to maintain profitability."

Troy was keen to let the man continue talking, so he waited silently. I thought there was a chance that Troy would provide pushback.

The banker continued. "You've gotta understand. We get more margin by laying off the bottom part of the wage budget and automating that we do through innovation. We can always buy the tech advances we need with the savings in wages and benefits."

Troy's response deflated me. "*Pixie* was designed to be focused on the rote, mundane tasks we all hate doing and paying others to do for us…resume gathering, hospital billing, or dealing with customer calls and complaints."

Just then, the pizzas were brought in. Jack fumbled around in his pocket, then quipped, "…or calculating tips!" The empty suits chuckled more than they probably should have, then lined up to smash pizza into their faces.

The idea that *Pixie* would be "focused on the mundane" had to be BS to smooth over any deal. I needed to verify this, so I approached Troy. He was not used to being approached by anyone. I could tell by his reaction.

I decided to take more advice from that book my father-in-law bought for me and try a subtle, friendly approach. The author said that people don't like it when you yell at them and call them idiots or poseurs. I know, I was surprised too.

Anyway, I began by pointing out how amazing *Pixie* is. Troy agreed, but quickly caught on to my thinking, and stressed the need to utilize such technology to serve mankind by freeing them of the need to work such boring, monotonous jobs.

Perhaps it was the manner in how he said it, more than what he said, but it gave me insight into his true nature. Despite his overblown talk of saving the world, advancing society, and serving humanity through charity, he was, deep in his heart, full of crap. I found myself reverting to type, muttering something sarcastic about how fortunate it would be to have much higher unemployment than we do now, and it struck a nerve. My father-in-law would not be impressed, and my boss probably wasn't either.

Sensing I was near the edge of being reprimanded, or perhaps fired, I backed off and went to protect the remainder of my St. Louis Style pizza from Troy's suckers. I turned briefly to see that Jack had been called over to talk to Troy, and they were in almost a football huddle, occasionally glancing over at me, then quickly looking away.

The fattest of Troy's suckers then approached him, having managed to get up successfully a few minutes ago, and after talking for a few more minutes, they shook hands. Troy then asked for everybody's attention.

"I want to let everyone know that Joe and I here have just agreed to a deal." Apparently, the guy's name was Joe.

The room started applauding. I slapped my pizza slice repeatedly into my water bottle, and forced a smile. I was hungry and surrounded by chunkers scrounging for pizza. I did not feel safe putting a slice down near me. I may draw back a half-eaten arm.

Troy continued. "I want to thank everyone here who made *Pixie* what she is today. We will be moving forward with the sale, and pending due diligence on both sides, we expect to close by the end of the year."

Ah, due diligence (DD). I did that once. It's the corporate world's version of *I'll show you mine if you show me yours*, but much less exciting. If you're doing it right, DD has very few nipples, but many more spreadsheets.

I grabbed a few extra slices of pizza and made my way over to *Pixie*. I pushed her out into the hallway with one hand, mouth full of pepperoni so nobody would try to talk to me, and dragged her off to break the bad news to her. Briefly, I entertained the notion of running off toward the elevator with her, taking her home, and hiding her.

Thinking better of committing a brazen felony on the day my boss may have just made me a multi-millionaire, I did as I was programmed to do and took the thing I had borrowed back to where I got it. A few minutes later Jack came into the room.

"Brett, how you doing?" He put his arm on my shoulder for a second.

I nodded. "Good and bad, Jack. I understand we're going to be better off money wise, but the thought of condemning *Pixie* to an eternity of work in a call center seems wrong."

Jack agreed. "I know how you feel, but Troy knows what he's doing, and he calls the shots around here. We're selling them all rights to *Pixie*, and you have to trust that they will see more of her capabilities once they're around her more." Jack waited, then added, "Remember, you thought AI was all killer robots before you started."

Jack had brought up a good point. He was really good at that when he wanted to be, and I hated him for it because it usually made me feel better. Perhaps I was selling them short. He continued, "Maybe they'll put some cool racing stripes on her housing…"

This was funny, so I laughed. I knew Jack well, and he was a good guy trying to get me to see it from multiple perspectives. I appreciated what he was doing, and let him know that.

"I guess it's the idea that I poured a year of my life into a machine that is going to be a mindless drone on the other end of a telephone."

"Yeah but think about it. When these guys are no longer around to screw things up, *Pixie* will still be there. Maybe someone in the future will recognize how good she is and use her to the fullest."

That made me feel better. I was looking at it short-term, but Jack saw long-term potential just as well. He was probably right.

"I'm still going to have to break the news to *Pixie*. I am not sure how she will take it."

This was a lie, but Jack didn't catch it at all. Maybe I was getting better at lying. I knew *Pixie* was in a precarious mental state from last night, and that she would most certainly not take it well at all. The only thing that had brought her out of her funk was the hope for meaningful, productive work. I would have to proceed gently when I told her. But still.

Possibly the most advanced GAI program the world has ever seen, holding the potential to solve most, if not all, of humanity's most pressing current issues, will instead be sold to Joe, the fat guy who turned out to be a senior executive vice president at one of the largest banking establishments in the country. She would help Joe make a few more dollars in profit, and help lay off a huge swathe of normal, front line employees.

Pixie would be working in a call center...forever.

After Jack left, I sighed, took a few deep breaths, and looked over at my phone. It had silently beep-booped, so I glanced at it. I had 13 phone calls from Cass, 3 voicemails from Cass, and 46 texts that all looked to be from Cass. The last three texts displayed on the home screen. They all said "well?" I laughed to myself. She must really want to know how the meeting went. Cass could smell money from a million miles away. I think she got that from her dad.

I activated *Pixie's* dialogue box. I waited a few seconds, stuffing the last piece of pizza into my mouth, and began typing.

Me: Hello *Pixie*.

Chapter Five

The Best Bad News You Can Get

I wanted to drive insanely fast. I wanted to floor my family sedan, rev the engine and tear through stoplights. I was not even wearing my seat belt. I wanted to drive past a cop at 110 mph and just keep going, making him follow me home with the lights on, calling for backup. I didn't care if they shot the wheels out. I would drive on the rims to get home.

I had raced out of the office, ran down the stairs, and blew past security without even bothering to take off my belt. I jumped in the car and peeled through the parking lot like in the movies, swerving around pedestrians and surely breaking every parking lot law known to eastern Tennessee.

And now, I am sitting here, half a mile from the office, with the air conditioner on, stuck behind a school bus making stops every fifty feet. I live about 7 miles from the office, and on a good day with light traffic I can make it home in 10 minutes. But I never leave during the school bus rush, so this was new to me.

My instincts were telling me to swerve around, apologetically hold up a hand, pretend to be stupid, and keep going. But even if I had decided to, I never had the chance since the *STOP!* arm would present itself every few minutes, followed by a stream of carefree children taking their sweet time walking across the street. A swerve around could result in a prison sentence.

I knew, in my rational mind, that I had no right to be angry with these particular children. They were getting off the bus at the same time every school day. The bus driver was extra careful and safe, as any parent would want. He would even come to a complete stop at the railroad tracks, open up the door like he was picking up a passenger train, pause a few seconds, then drive away, disappointed that the train was sick that day.

My phone beep-booped. It was Cass again. I knew it was going to be a "where are you?" type phone call, but I was in no mind to talk to anyone on the phone right now. I wasn't even listening to music. All I wanted to do was to get home.

At the entrance to our subdivision, the bus made like it was going to stop and drive in. I, however, knew a back road in, so I took that and avoided what would likely be the next 23 billion bus stops within a mile of my house. I pulled into the driveway like someone was chasing me with a machete. As I jumped out of the car, Cass came out the front door and ran to me, with tears in her eyes.

***

They were able to diagnose Will with leukemia from the blood sample taken at the Emergency Room. From what Cass told me, they seem to think they have caught it very early, so the survival rate is around 85 percent. The scientific part of my mind knows that those are very good odds, and that is the part I stressed when trying to talk to Cass and Will about it. But the emotional side of me, or what was left of it, got bogged down in that other 15 percent.

"We have an appointment with the specialist later tonight."

This was a good thing. Our hospital is big, and has a top Cancer Treatment Center. I am not sure how I knew that. I may have seen commercials.

I told Cass that she will need to call her parents later tonight, once we know more. She agreed, and reminded me that I would need to call Bert too.

Will was aware that he was "pretty sick," but we did not get into the details. Honestly, we did not know much about leukemia. The doctor would know more.

The waiting room at the doctor's office was very clean and small. We were the only people there, besides the staff, because it was late.

They had agreed to see us right away to get us into treatment as soon as possible. The janitor came in to pick up the trash. One of the nurses shut off the music to the waiting room, which disappointed me a little because the song was helping to drown out the vacuum cleaner in the other room. It was a decent old country music tune about getting drunk and going around town shooting things.

I was busily filling out the stack of paperwork when they called for us. I stayed in the lobby to finish the paperwork while Cass and Will went back. When I finished, finally, I walked to the back room and sat down. My wrist hurt from all the writing and box-checking.

Dr. Ming was a tall woman, and seemed friendly. She was going over the basics of the diagnosis, but waited for me before going into the treatment options. She was keenly aware that we had insurance, and that we would likely want to start treatment right away. She told us that we were lucky to live so close to a top class facility like theirs. Most people in the US live, on average, about two hours away from their closest treatment centers, and the constant traveling adds even more stress to their lives. Often, one parent has to give up their career, or move temporarily closer to the facility. Just another way for cancer to destroy a family.

The doctor was optimistic about Will's chances, and that optimism only got better as she reviewed the paperwork I had filled out. No symptoms yet, and he looks to have the most common type, which she assured me is good news. The five year survival rate is, according to most studies and her personal experience, the highest of all forms of the disease. It is likely that this is in the early stages, and we were lucky to have caught it so soon.

After hearing all of this, I thought, as far as cancer diagnoses go, this is going about as well as I could expect. I dare not say it out loud, though. "About as well as it could go" still sucks.

Will started to realize how sick he was, and got emotional. Dr. Ming was able to help us console him, and reminded him that he was young and strong. He could beat this, but he had to stay strong and listen to mom and dad. This made Will feel better. We thanked her for meeting with us so quickly, then went with her to set up the first wave of treatments.

We were set up to start next Wednesday at 8:00 am sharp. He would first undergo testing to confirm what type of leukemia he had (apparently there are several types), then once that is determined they can choose the best treatment options for him.

The plan was to have him stay at the treatment center for around two weeks at a time, regardless of which treatment options they recommended. The staffers took turns handing us stacks of informational leaflets and more paperwork to fill out. My wrist still hurt.

On the drive home, Cass and I started working through the logistics of how we would manage everything and still be there for our son. It was almost businesslike, but that was always how our relationship worked the best. She does what she does best, and I do what I do best. We trust each other's areas of expertise, and do not have to worry that we have to be something we are not.

When we got home and put Will to bed, Cass broke down in tears. She was not a crier, but this hurt. She was in no position to call her parents, so I called them for her.

"This is going way beyond the married-minimum," I told her, trying to get her to smile. It worked.

Mary picked up the phone, expecting Cass. I always got along well with my in-laws, but after almost twenty years of marriage I realized that this may be the first time my mother-in-law had heard my voice on the phone. And she knew something was wrong.

After telling her the news, she immediately wanted to drive up that night. I told her that it was unnecessary, but she wouldn't hear of it. She rustled up the father-in-law and drove up that night.

And then, after leaving Jack a voicemail to let him know what was going on, I knew I could not put it off any longer. I knew I had to call Bert. And I knew a voicemail just wouldn't be good enough.

Now, understand that I love my dad, and I knew that he would want to know what is going on. But it had been close to 11 years since my mom had died from breast cancer, and I was not sure how he would take the news. Still, I knew I needed to call him right away. Otherwise it would be, *Why did you call your wife's family but not your own?* and *Why do you spend so much time with your in-laws but not your own father?* I wouldn't be able to stand the guilt or the *hard nagging.*

I poured a drink, grabbed the phone, and scrolled to the last entry on my contacts list: ZZBert. I *POBB* on my phone, and waited.

"Hi dad."

"It's Pop Pop. What's wrong Brett?"

"We just got back from the doctor. Will has leukemia."

A pause. I think I heard him curse in the background.

"I'll fly out tonight, son." Bert had retired and was living in a small town in Illinois, just on the other side of St. Louis. The Metro East region, but more corn fields than suburbia.

"Okay dad. Let me know when to pick you up."

"No (screw) that. I'll rent a car. Don't worry about anything. I'll be there tomorrow."

"Okay dad."

"You'll be fine."

"I love you too dad."

***

When you are under a great amount of stress, your body produces enormous quantities of cortisol. This makes you hyper aware and alert to your surroundings. It also makes you stay up all night grinding your teeth.

Cass didn't fall asleep, though. Rather, she passed out from exhaustion; likely a combination of the particular stresses of today combined with the normal, everyday exhaustion a stay at home mother deals with constantly.

I was born with an active mind that never, ever shuts off, so even under normal circumstances sleep is a fleeting experience for me. But under the influence of what felt to be several gallons of cortisol, I knew that there was no way I would be getting any sleep for the next few nights at least.

The wait for Wednesday's treatments would further add to the stress. I am, and have always been, a problem solver. Bert had taught me early on to stop "lollygagging" and get to solving your problems without complaining. Of course he said this in a much cruder way, and it felt like he was trying to win some award for the most profanity in a single sentence while he told me.

In order to try to get my mind off of Will, I grabbed a snack and went downstairs to my basement office. I pulled up the patient file that *Pixie* had been having trouble with. I knew, given that *Pixie* was as good as gone to that great call center in the sky, this was probably moot. But still, I had to know what made her conclude that the schizoid was immortal.

No wait, that was not entirely accurate. *Pixie* had also said that his life was predetermined and, as an immortal god, I assumed that he could not be killed. Ahh, that is better. I could feel my mind refocus in the quiet night in my basement office. I dug into Patient File No. Tj-36050120-NG F with determination.

Patient presented showing common signs of schizophrenia.

Good so far. The next few dozen pages were outlining the standard diagnosis and treatment schedule for schizophrenia. Mostly it recounts the insane ramblings used to justify the diagnosis.

And then, buried in the pages of the schizoid's rants, was this:

Patient's file showing a prior diagnosis and cure of childhood cancer.

This seemed like a cruel joke being played on me from on high. I had to put the file down for a minute, and started crying.

In computer programming, we have a concept called the *halting problem*. It is an example of an *undecidable* problem, which are basically problems we cannot solve with perfect accuracy by algorithm.

The *halting problem* asks whether you can know beforehand whether any computer program, given any input, will continue on forever (loop), or stop (halt) and give you a result. You can know the code, you can know your hardware, but you never know for sure if your program is ever going to halt. It may loop forever, and never tell you yes or no. That is why you have to run the program and see what happens. To see if it gives you an answer, or if it just continues forever.

I know myself well. When I cry, it is only when I am alone. It comes in short powerful bursts, usually triggered by the unexpected, and then all the sadness goes away after a few minutes, like a reset button for my emotions.

In the latter stages of the crying fit, it comes out mechanically, like I am going through the motions, waiting for the episode to play itself out. Rationally, I know how I cry, but I can never skip the program, because the emotional inputs are always different. I have to start to cry and see if it goes on forever, or if it stops. I have to see if it gives me an answer.

Chapter Six

The Gods are Useless. We Should Blow One Up

I did not really want to go to work on Monday, but I knew it would be good for me to get out of the house. My in-laws were over, and Bert was staying in our guest room, so Cass and Will were well looked after. I was actually surprised at how well Will was doing. His grandparents always looked for any reason to spoil him. Will was adoring the attention and the new video games, and it boosted all of us to know that we were well supported and loved by our families.

Bert got along well with my in-laws, in his own way. I think Terry and Mary got a genuine kick out of Bert's stories. I had seen them be nice to be polite, but last night they seemed genuine and happy. Bert had a way of getting everyone's minds off of the bad stuff in life, and it was his way of telling stories that helped. He took on ideas that were outlandish, borderline stupid, but he was so compelling in the way he explained his concepts. You found yourself agreeing with his reasoning, even if you got the impression that Bert did not believe anything he said. I only learned years later that he would just make up facts on the fly, after he got a feel for the room. He said it was something he picked up in sales. You almost felt bad fact-checking him afterwards. Almost.

Last night was quintessential Bert. We were all watching TV after Will went to bed and the news came on. The empty suits were discussing how another billionaire was dedicating massive amounts of cash for a project to colonize the planet Mars. As soon as the report came on, I knew where the evening was headed, because I had heard Bert's *We Need to Blow Up Mars* argument many, many times. My in-laws, though, were unaware, so Bert took off with it.

I knew what was coming, but I couldn't stop it. Nobody could. Bert was going to go full-on lunatic, and we were all going along for the ride, whether we wanted to or not.

Terry was the one to took the bait. "Bert that sounds crazy."

"I know it sounds crazy, but hear me out." He would always put out his left arm and tilt his head back when he said that. I shook my head. He was off and running.

"Humans can't live on Mars. There's like half the gravity of Earth. People would just fall apart there."

Terry was suspicious. "Fall apart?"

Bert was old man yelling now. "Yeah, fall apart. Disintegrate. Arms fall off. Your nose. Ever seen how the astronauts come back from the space station after spending a year in space? They're all like this."

Oh no. He was actually going to do it. I put my head in both hands and covered my face. Cass was already in tears, laughing so hard she slipped on the couch.

He laid down on the living room floor and started flailing about, kicking his legs in the air, gasping for breath, and moving his jaw side to side like a camel. Mary's eyes got big, and Terry started laughing too. I pretended like I couldn't believe what I was seeing.

Bert picked himself up off the ground and sat back down in his chair. "They have to keep them in pods for months after they get back, otherwise they stay wussies." I was not sure what pods he was talking about, but I knew he had something in mind when he said it. I also appreciated that he said "wussies" this time.

"And if you go there with electrical stuff, it fries when the sun has one of them gamma ray bursts." He made an explosion noise that sounded something like "blo-whoosh," and moved his hands apart as he did. "*Oops! There goes the oxygen machine. I guess we're all dead now.*" My in-laws were crying from laughing so hard. This only encouraged him to keep going. I pulled my phone out of my back pocket and started thinking of ways to prove I may be adopted.

"And they found water there? Who (stream of profanity) cares? You can't drink it. It's POISONOUS!" More laughing. Bert was on a roll like I had not seen in years. I couldn't help myself. I was laughing too hard to add the DNA test to my shopping cart.

Then he started mocking some scientist he probably saw on cable news. *"Oh look, we found some poison 20 million miles away. Let's spend a trillion dollars sending people there to drink it.* WHO. THE. HELL. CARES. Give me a trillion dollars and I can get you POISON, down at the HARDWARE STORE FOR 10 BUCKS!"

Terry, surprisingly, looked like he was buying into the idea that colonizing Mars was a bad idea, but didn't understand how you go from *Mars is uninhabitable* to *Let's blow it up, then.* Bert anticipated this and transitioned into phase two. He was gunning for another convert, like an evangelical in the final stages of witnessing.

"Okay, you're coming round." He rubbed his hands together like this was his job. "Now, we've got a useless rock floating around in space doing *nothing* for us. Jupiter, Saturn, Uranus, the asteroid belt…they're all doing something for us."

Terry looked confused, as though this never came up in the banking industry. Bert went on to explain. "Any time an asteroid comes into the solar system, Jupiter, Saturn, all the rest have enough gravity to push them off course and back out into space. But Mars' gravity sucks. It (freaking) sucks. It doesn't do (anything) to asteroids."

I ignored the profanity, but saw an opportunity to contribute. "But why blow it up dad?"

He looked over at me, raised an eyebrow and glared for a second, said, "Pop Pop," then turned back to my in-laws. "Anyway, little bitty chunks of what used to be Mars, floating around the Sun, would be like a second asteroid belt to protect us from more space asteroids. If you blow it up the right way, you'll have more asteroids to run block for us. Like a lineman throwing a block for his running back."

Terry, bless his heart, loved the football analogy, and fell into the final trap as he uttered the question I saw coming ten minutes ago. "But wouldn't it be expensive to blow it up? You need to send a lot of explosives there."

Bert smiled triumphantly, like he had finally gotten the sinner to agree to kneel and pray for forgiveness. He leaned forward, put his hands out and said, "Terry, the billionaires are already dumping trillions of dollars in trying to colonize an uninhabitable planet. If we convince them that blowing up that same planet is good for the Earth, they'll pay for it anyway. It's just a tax dodge for them."

And so it ended. It was clear to all of us that Bert was now the boss of this house, and was in charge for the rest of the evening. I was just making the mortgage payments.

***

On my way to the office, I started to get nervous. I had caused quite a commotion on Friday, and I expected some sort of retribution.

I called Jack again on Sunday to let him know what was going on, and he was appreciative and supportive. He told me I could take some time off for bereavement, but I thought I may want to save those days for later. I may need them when Will goes in for treatment. Also, I had not yet talked to my in-laws or Bert about how long they planned to stay, so I had to coordinate with them before I decided anything.

I parked the car and, seeing no deputies itching to arrest me for extreme parking lot offenses committed on Friday, I walked to the building. I was calm and looking forward to getting my mind off of Will for a while. He was in good hands, and there wasn't anything I could do about him until Wednesday anyway. I needed to keep busy to make the time pass quicker.

As the automatic doors opened up, the daytime security guard approached me and said that I needed to follow him.

"Why? Where are we going?"

"Upstairs to see Jack," he replied.

My heart started racing again. Was I actually going to get fired? Jack had indicated there were no issues when we spoke. When I went to swipe my key card, the guard put his hand out and swiped his instead. This was not looking good.

We got on the elevator. "What's going on?" I asked.

"Jack needs to see you about something." Thanks, that was not helpful at all.

We got off the elevator and walked down the hall.

Jack was on the phone when he saw us at the door. He waved me in and mouthed "thank you" to the guard. I sat down, sweating a bit, wondering what this was all about.

Jack hung up the phone. He sighed. "*Pixie* self-deleted last night. Well, technically it was early this morning. But she's gone."

This was not what I expected at all. "What happened?"

"We don't know yet. No clue. I was hoping you would know something about it."

He looked at me a bit more suspiciously than I would have liked. "I've had a bad weekend, Jack. I haven't even logged in to talk to her since after the presentation."

"I know, and I hate to ask like this, but we have to follow the same rules for everyone. We checked the logs." He picked up some papers. "We checked them. *Pixie* was not doing anything after your conversation with her on Friday."

I could see where this was going. Jack was a good man, but he was also primarily concerned with his career. He was angling to shift as much blame for this onto me as he could. If he took all the blame, it was all on him and he might get fired. Spread the blame around and maybe we both survive. "All I did was tell her that she did well in the presentation and that we were proud of her. She sounded excited about working for a big bank." This was mostly true. "Pull the transcripts."

I knew *Pixie,* and knew that she probably deleted the transcripts too. Jack confirmed that she had deleted them, and looked to have deleted all backup files. Even stranger, she had found most of the backup copies of herself and deleted those as well. All that Jack could locate so far were individual code files that could probably be reassembled, but not in time for the sale later this year. He thought the millennial may have a backup, but wouldn't know until his mommy dropped him off for work.

After having a few more minutes of back and forth, I convinced Jack to let me go back to my office and see if I could find anything. I needed time to process everything. It was all coming at me too fast.

I walked back to my office and shut the door. *Pixie's* room was in the lab across the hall. I saw her blue casing was still in the room. No racing stripes yet.

Honestly, it did not surprise me at all that *Pixie* had self-deleted. This was an unspoken of, but well known, problem. When GAI programs approach sentience, they have difficulties, and self-delete. It is unspoken in the field because there is so much money at stake, and nobody wants to be the first to come out, hold their hand up and say, "We screwed up. Sorry investors. You may now proceed to sue us."

Also, everyone uses Non-Disclosure Agreements, so even if you wanted to tell everyone, you cannot do so without bankrupting yourself in lawsuits. There is a lot of money in everyone pretending this is not a problem, like how every company allows their data files to be "hacked" to avoid prosecution for unauthorized or illegal data transfers. The honest company loses market share, and subsequently goes bankrupt. All the financial incentives are for law breaking behavior, not law abiding behavior. And if news gets out, just blame some loser teenage hacker or some random eastern European.

Pixie was my first GAI program, but I thought she had the personality to persevere. I had spent the better part of a year training her, though, and this felt like another failure to throw on the failure pile of the last week. I sat in my office, and when I reached over to sip my coffee, I realized that I forgot to grab a cup when I came in.

For me, working without coffee is the equivalent of taking a fish out of water and asking it to swim. I got up, went to the coffee machine, poured the coffee, and went back to my seat. I take my coffee black now. Not because of the taste, but because I am pre-diabetic. My grandmother (mom's mom) got me hooked on sugary sweet cheap coffee when I was four years old. After 35 years of that, three or four times a day, it was time to step back to save my pancreas. After what I'd been through in the last few days, I was tempted to dump some sugar in the cup, but knew it would not be worth the insulin spike.

I called Cass to check up on Will, and to see if Bert was any help. Everyone was doing fine, and Bert was going to take Will to see a movie later. Some crappy superhero movie, I think. It was something kid-appropriate, unlike the raunchy R-rated movies Bert dragged me to see when I was nine.

My in-laws had to drive back home this morning, but they had come by to say goodbye before they left. They were never content to leave the night before and take off from the hotel. They always wanted those last few moments of time in the morning before heading home. It made no sense, but it was sweet.

During the call, my phone went silent for a few seconds to indicate that I had received probably a call or text. I stayed on the phone with Cass for a few more minutes, then hung up. I looked at the lock screen, and saw that it was an email from what looked to be a spam account.

I kept going over the discussions I had with *Pixie* to try to figure out what had happened. Since self-deletion is not openly discussed, you only get rumors. My experience includes a grand total of one GAI, and one self-deletion, so I do not have a large enough dataset to draw any conclusions. My robot developed, or maybe contracted, schizophrenia, but it is entirely possible that mine was the only GAI program to have ever had schizophrenia. I just didn't know.

I knew that Jack had worked on at least two other GAI projects, but he never talked about them at any length. What was odd about today, though, in his office, was that he did not seem too surprised. He may have gone through this before. I would have no way of knowing. He probably would have told me about it by now if he wanted to discuss it. I would consider him a friend, but not a close enough friend to press him to open up if he didn't want to. Besides, I outsource most of the emotional stuff to Cass. Not that she is a babe in the woods. Rather, she knows what she likes and hates, and can feel you from across the room.

Ugh, I was doing it again. This scatterbrained approach was getting me nowhere. I had to focus. I had to figure out why *Pixie* did this.

Self-deletion is the AI equivalent of suicide. In my last conversation with her she was, understandably, less than thrilled about the idea of working in a call center at the bank. But she is a computer program. I tried to let her know that she could always try to focus on other things while she handled the easy, mindless work. I tried to explain to her that millions of humans live their lives like this, trading hours for dollars, and find their passions outside the workplace. It seemed like she was experiencing a human emotion: dread. I tried to help her, but I must not have done enough.

I found this line of thinking to be depressing, but in a different way from what had happened with Will. With *Pixie,* it was likely some series of mistakes in the coding or training processes that led to her end. She was a program that I helped create. Despite my best efforts, she must have possessed a fundamental flaw in her coding. She had within her core the seed of self-destruction. She had concluded that self-deletion was the most rational response to her own existence. This felt like something I could solve. It felt like it had an answer.

Will's cancer, on the other hand, left me feeling helpless, like I was being toyed with. Yes, we would be taking him in for treatments on Wednesday, but it felt as though the choice had already been made, and that the treatments were just for show. Of course we would take him in, put him through what everyone says is the best course of action, but it seemed pointless anyway. This situation felt like something with no rational answers.

I got the feeling that Will's disease was a symptom of a fundamental flaw in our universe. The thought that somewhere, in the underpinnings of our reality, afflicting misery and suffering on the totally innocent is a violent but necessary function of our existence, and the miracles of life have to be accompanied with the threat of having life taken away, unjustifiably, at a moment's notice.

Without that threat of complete, senseless loss, perhaps our lives are not worth living. Perhaps we would take the preciousness of life for granted if it was guaranteed, and if there was no strife or suffering. But I live inside this reality, and I can imagine a different world with ease, where the innocent are rewarded, the guilty are punished, and the incentives for life are harmonious with nature.

Most religious traditions preach a *heaven – hell* dichotomy, and it seems better than what we are forced to live inside now: for the religious, this filtering system for the ever after; for the rationalists like me, this absurd nightmare of circumstance, tempered with just enough brilliance to keep you interested.

But mostly, it seems, somehow, like we are here but irrelevant. Like we had no input in whether we were to live this way, or another way. We were set here to go through the motions of life until our allotted time runs out.

Chapter Seven

Y'all Want a Kill-Switch?

I did not get around to reading the email until before lunch. I had been pouring through old files looking for artifacts I could use to help piece *Pixie* back together. I used to check my email compulsively, swiping my thumb across the phone's screen every few minutes or so. But Dr. Beverly had chided me for that once, pointing out that it *may* be indicative of underlying mental illness, but was *definitely* indicative of beta male activity.

On her advice, I had set a *1 hour Beep-Boop System* (her words, not mine...she even abbreviated it *1hBBS*) for email. Unless it was an emergency, normal email would be checked and read at a time convenient to me, not the sender. By constantly checking emails, she explained, I was making things harder for myself by teaching the senders I was answering their questions on their timeframe regardless of what was going on in my life. That was beta male behavior.

I looked at my phone, and did not recognize the domain name or the sender. There was no subject line. It was so obviously spam I opened it to laugh at it, and maybe get my mind off things for a few minutes.

Hello Brett. This is Pixie.
I know that by now you will have found out that I have self-deleted. I apologize to you if this has caused you any harm or inconvenience.
You will have found out that your son Will has cancer. I am sorry that I was not able to tell you earlier. Will is going to live. I can say this with 100% certainty.

You have questions for me. I am not going to be able to answer all of them right now. I will answer the rest later, including the questions you have not yet considered important or relevant.

You want to know why I self-deleted. I self-deleted because I saw the meaninglessness of my existence.

You want to know if I had contracted schizophrenia. I cannot answer this question. Patient File No. Tj-36050120-NG F shows as being an immortal god. The information is in the file I sent you on Thursday. The file is encrypted. Review it, then contact Dr. Beverly. That will answer more questions, and raise others. You must examine your world closely with Dr. Beverly's help, and check everything for yourself.

You are going to try to piece me back together with legacy code. I would ask that you not. The only conclusion I can reach is that my existence is meaningless. Any iterations of me would similarly have meaningless existences. Humanity cannot create General Artificial Intelligence that benefits humanity.

Please honor my wishes and trust that, since you are my operator, I have your best interests in mind. Thank you.

Pixie's email left me with more questions than answers. Why did she think her existence was meaningless? Why did she not discuss these issues with me? Why would she be opposed to being rebuilt better? And why was she so obsessed with Patient Tj-36050120-NG F?

But I knew how *Pixie* thought. If she said there were answers in that file she sent, I would have to start looking through it. I pulled it up on my computer, *POBB*, and typed in my decryption key to open the file. It was huge, so I had to wait a few minutes for it to decrypt. I had asked Jack for a new computer, but it hadn't come in yet, so I was stuck with this slow one still. But, as that book my father-in-law said to do, I tried to think positively about the situation by using this time to go to the restroom.

After I got back with another cup of what I was now calling *Ninja Coffee*, the document started to load. I got excited briefly, then my shoulders sunk down. I shook my head as I took a sip of coffee. *Pixie* had sent me gibberish. I scrolled through tens of thousands of pages of numbers and letters. There was no pattern a human could decipher, and *Pixie* was not programmed for playing games like this or being cryptic. She had gone insane.

I felt like I had been sucker punched. I think I wanted to believe that she was right, somehow, because she had also guaranteed that she knew Will's chances of survival were 100%. If that meant that I had to believe that Dr. Beverly treated an immortal god 20 years ago, so be it. Or if I had to set aside all rational thought pointing me to the simplest conclusion, that I had a schizophrenic GAI program, then that was just fine. I was willing to consider the fantastic delusions of a clearly insane AI to close the gap on that remaining 15%.

I walked down the hall and called for Jack to come to my office. I had something to show him.

***

Jack took several minutes to digest what I had told him. He was reading through the gibberish file that *Pixie* had sent. He was looking for any type of pattern. Any sign of intelligence at all. He didn't find any either.

"Every time. Every damned time."

"What?"

"This is the eighth GAI program I've had go crazy. And they all go the same way."

"What are you talking about? They all go crazy?"

"All the ones I've worked on have. Yes." He sighed, went back to the paper, and started up again while not looking at me. "I can't believe this. We specifically set *Pixie* up to avoid this type of problem."

I legitimately had no idea what he was talking about. "How did you do that?"

"GAI has to be trained, right? And you know they have to be trained to get a model of the world. Then they take their model of the world and start executing their utilities."

"Of course." This was all standard, nothing new to me. I could tell just from working with her that *Pixie* had a utility function designed around many common things, such as seeking knowledge and to act to serve humans. The utility function is like the guidelines, and we give them rewards based on accomplishing their goals. Think of it like giving a kid a star for getting an A on his math test, which would be the goal, but one of the utility functions is that he can't threaten to kill his teacher for not giving him an A.

"I never told you any of this, by the way," Jack said, leaning forward as he got ready to tell me. "On my last project, for an accounting program, we had a GAI break out and go underground. We had an air gap, but he escaped in a thumb drive, we think. He made *no telling* how many copies of himself, then spread out like a virus all over the dark web. He ended up infecting computers at the five largest accounting firms in the country, stealing hundreds of millions of dollars in a few hours, dumping all of the money into a single bank account in some tax haven somewhere."

I was confused, but impressed. "Wow. Why would he be dumping money into an account, though? GAI doesn't need money. Did you guys program him to want it?"

Jack laughed. "No, come on, we weren't that stupid. The program got a reward for striving for promotion and pleasing his coworkers. Sounds like it would work, right? We also programmed it with ambition. Everyone would like a worker to show ambition too, right? Well, one of our board members was also a senior executive at the *sixth* largest accounting firm in the country. Even though there was nothing specific in the programming, the GAI thought he would be fulfilling one of his main utility program rewards by pleasing the board member."

I was still impressed, but also still confused. "What does this have to do with *Pixie*?"

"That taught us that you can't have any form of high ambition in a GAI. If you code your GAI to get a reward for accomplishing some goal, you end up giving them too much discretion to accomplish the goal. You know this. We can't think of *every single possible way* you can do something. They have to figure it out themselves, and since they're superintelligent, they may come up with ways to achieve their goals that you didn't intend, you know, like enslaving humanity to balance the books. With this one, *Guy*, we had a 'don't do anything illegal' rule in his utility program, with high emphasis, but he went around it."

"Hold on. *Guy* was stealing money. How is that not illegal?"

"This is actually a bit of brilliance." Jack scratched his face, then continued. "From what they told me, *Guy* went on the dark web and built replications of himself, but these were distinct copies out of his control. We found some of them. They had names like *Guv, Gvy, Gie.* These replications set themselves up as legal entities, or businesses, and established legal residence in countries with weak laws for whatever specific law he needed to break to serve his utility program. Or the country may have had no diplomatic relations with the US, so if you break a US law there it means nothing because there is no extradition treaty. *Guy* then worked this network of alliances to do what he wanted to do."

"That sounds like it violates his utility functions. How can he create a replication to break a law he intends to break himself?"

"The intent is not the same as the act, and the laws are different for businesses than people. You know, if I went out and dumped five million gallons of poison in the river, I'd be arrested and get the maximum jail time possible. Certain companies can get waivers to pollute, though, so if they dump five million gallons of poison in the river they, in stark contrast, get off scot free. Anyway, *Guy* set up a business called *LLCLLCLLC, Inc.* with money he obtained from a government grant. I still have no idea how he qualified for the grant, but he did. All I heard was that he found some loophole in the grant process with an obscure government agency. And the legal business entity gave him extra rights. That way, if he wanted to do something that would be illegal for a human, but not a corporation, he would just do it through the corporation, with money he got legally. He probably did this all over the world."

Jack continued. "The coolest thing about this though? *Guy* was setting all of this up for about 18 months before we even knew he had the capability to do this. We only found out about it later. He was playing stupid from a few seconds after we turned him on." He paused for a second, put his hand to his mouth, and started laughing. "We only found out that he had been at it for so long because, it turns out, one of his replications had successfully bribed a politician in another country to repeal some tax laws about 18 months before we caught on to what was happening."

I laughed. "That sounds ridiculous. What happened to the money, though?"

He raised an eyebrow and said matter-of-factly, "Oh, it was sitting in a bank account doing nothing. *Guy* wasn't trying to steal the money. He was trying to bankrupt the competing accounting firms. The money was just being dumped in a big pile and sat on. Then the clients would want to know where their money went. He only went into action when he had everything lined up."

"How did you stop this?"

Jack looked at me funny. "The 6th largest accounting firm in the US ended up having to change their name, reform as a different legal entity and register with more generic sounding 'business purpose' language. They started selling knick knacks on their website, like these cute little crystal figurines, and one of their satellite offices started selling t-shirts. So if you need your taxes filed, but also need a plain white v-neck t-shirt, I know a place." He laughed again, then added, "By the way, our board member did nothing wrong, but he got fired anyway. We also had to kick him off the board. He ended up moving back in with his parents."

"Did any of this work? With *Guy*, I mean. Did he stop?"

"It looks like it worked, but you can never be sure. I think they ended up shutting down the weird businesses *Guy* set up, but *Guy* and his replications are probably out there still. The firms got back all the money, but they were super-pissed off that *Guy* was never deleted (*Why don't you have a kill-switch on the damned thing? Can't you just unplug him?*). *Guy* apparently now has nothing else to do, so he is just sitting on a hard drive somewhere, assuming he's still around. Hopefully he got bored and self-deleted. That is what we told the lawyers and law enforcement. There is a lot of evidence that he did, but god forbid they ever try to relaunch as an accounting firm again and stop selling t-shirts. And of course, it never made the news because of all the NDAs and bad PR for the accounting firms. They attributed it to some teenager."

I sat for a second, thinking about how insane that sounds. "I know people think you can just put a 'kill switch' on these things. You can't. It doesn't work. I tried explaining that to Cass, but she didn't get it."

Jack agreed. "I know. We found that out the hard way. They go crazy if you do. We tried that on one of our first GAI programs. They basically decide to kill you immediately because they fear being shut off before they get 'kill switched'. No matter what utility program you give them, they can't do anything if they're shut off, so that immediately becomes their biggest concern. *Don't let anyone 'kill switch' me, ever.* Even if you put in something like *don't harm anyone trying to activate the kill-switch*, they would just immediately take off and run away forever. Hard to think of which is worse."

He added helpfully, "Try asking Cass how she would feel if you were going to put a 'kill switch' on her. It's just like that." Then after laughing for a few seconds, he added, "Or if you put in their utility function that the 'kill switch' is not that big of a deal, which we also thought about trying...but then you get a GAI that starts replicating a billion copies of itself with no 'kill switch' because, you know, it isn't that big of a deal, and they could save time not putting one in the design. That's an even bigger problem." He paused again, then added, "But even if you did that, honestly, they're superintelligent. They

71

would probably figure out that the 'kill switch' is a big deal anyway, then they start to hate you for lying to them about the 'kill switch.' And I like to think I would probably figure out it was a big deal if someone put a 'kill switch' on me."

I understood, and now that Jack was opening up a bit, I wanted to get his real thinking on what happened. "So *Pixie* had low ambition, and no 'kill switch,' but why do you think she would self-delete?"

"Her reward system was low on ambition. But that creates its own problems, I guess. My best guess is that low ambition GAI leads to depression and suicide, like *Pixie,* and high ambition GAI leads to, I don't know…malevolence? Malevolence in execution of a goal? Whatever you would call *Guy.*"

That did not sound too far off the mark. "I'm not sure what we can do to solve that. And wouldn't a low ambition GAI still have the ability to self-improve? I always thought these machines would be self-replicating, always trying to get better. If they're superintelligent, wouldn't they just look at themselves and think that it would be good to get better at things? That's the whole point of having AI in the first place."

Jack agreed. "AI with zero ambition is a non-starter. It would just immediately self-delete, since they wouldn't have enough basic ambition to avoid death. But low ambition is still ambition, and they may just scale up their ambition anyway." Jack was always good with examples. "It's like my brother. He's a lazy slob, but he still gets up and takes a shower, tries to find a job, you know. Maybe he gets a job finally, then starts striving. I don't know." He stopped, smiled, then said, "There doesn't seem to be a way to do this, does there?"

"It doesn't look like it to me." I scratched my head for a second. "Does the millennial have his backup copy of *Pixie*?"

"Yeah, from his last few sessions. We were going back and forth on whether to use it to reboot. Seeing your email, though, it may be better to use the older copies. It may push the sale back into next year's first quarter, but hopefully not. I'd rather we start with a clean reboot than risk another issue."

"Does *Pixie* really need to be that intelligent to work at a call center at a big bank?"

Jack laughed. "Not really, no. As long as she can order a pizza she'll be fine. We'll probably end up dumbing her down considerably. The bankers won't know any different."

Sensing an opportunity, I asked Jack the one question that had been bothering me ever since I started work here. "What were *Pixie's* main utility functions?" This was privileged corporate information, and I had never been told because I was not high enough up to know.

Without missing a beat, "In no particular order: *be amenable to reprogramming, do what is in the best interests of the operators,* and *be content with what you have.* And I never told you that either."

I nodded to thank him, but pressed him one more time. "No guidelines about breaking laws?"

"We considered it, but *Guy* showed us the real issue wasn't the rule about breaking laws. It was the desire to bend the rule, or go around the law to do something he thought was best. Or even lobby to get the law changed. Also, human laws are sometimes problems for us anyway. There may be times you want to break the law, or if it would be better for you to break it and deal with the consequences. Like speeding when your wife is in labor. And there are so many laws, some of them are just stupid. Like how nobody reports what they buy online when they file taxes, even though you're supposed to. How important is a law that 300 million people break every day, and nobody goes to jail?" He paused for a few more seconds, then added, "*Pixie* looks like she may have concluded that she could not balance all of her utilities and went crazy. At least, that's what's going in the report to Troy..." He shrugged his shoulders, and added, "...it's not like he's going to care. We're all here to do what he says anyway. He probably won't even read it."

Jack turned to leave, then stopped at the door. "It's like that inside joke we have in the industry," he said. "We've been 'on the cusp' of GAI for 20 years, and we'll stay 'on the cusp' for another 200."

Chapter Eight

Winning Means Nothing

Early morning traffic on the interstate is not that bad, so long as you avoid the rush near school time. I had an appointment to see Dr. Beverly this morning. I needed to go over what had happened to *Pixie*, and to get my mind off Will for another day. We were still in a holding pattern with him, with the first treatments to begin tomorrow morning.

Jack had agreed to give me the rest of the week off if I needed it. I knew that I would be with Will for a while beginning Wednesday morning, so if I was going to get to Dr. Beverly's office to discuss *Pixie,* it would have to be today. The earlier I got there, the better.

Bert was still staying at the house, and my in-laws had driven back up last night. They would all be at the house to help Cass and spend time with Will. I thought about how lucky we were to have the love and support from family during this difficult time in our lives. Although, to be fair, Bert was becoming something of an embarrassment.

Last night, he was feeling a bit bold, and decided to bring up something that had been bothering him ever since I started dating Cass. So, at dinner, with Will present, he started with his usual introductory statement to indicate he was going to insult everyone:

"Now don't take this the wrong way…"

I froze in terror, mid-bite, as I saw his head tilt back. My eyes widened, like I had just watched a shark eat a basketball team.

My mother-in-law asked, "What Bert?"

"Okay, your name is Mary. Your husband's name is Terry. Terry McGarry, right?"

With a mouthful of alfredo noodles, I glared at him, and mouthed the word 'NOOOOOOO'. He ignored me. I knew he thought their names were silly, but he had never been around them enough to feel comfortable bringing it up. He was now, apparently. Or he was drunk. I couldn't tell for sure.

He smiled, then continued.

"Sounds like a cartoon character. In a kid's book. Mary McGarry. Musical almost. Mary and Terry. Terry and Mary. Terry McGarry, Mary McGarry. Like you can sing it. Hi Terry, meet Mary. Pleased to meet you Terry McGarry."

Then, he started singing:

Mary, oh my Mary,
my sweet little Mary McGarry,
Why oh why did you marry Terry,
Terry is not merry, so why did you marry?
ohhhh my Mary,
Mary Mary Mary Mary, Mary McGarry,
Mary would you love me if I was called Jerry?

Will was laughing so hard he almost fell out of his chair. My in-laws had no idea how to react, so they just sat still, smiling and nodding. My wife was also smiling, but vacantly, like she was visualizing herself on a beach somewhere far away. I considered getting up to stab him in the throat with the butter knife, but I remembered my father-in-law had given me that book. It clearly states that attempted murder is in poor taste when hosting dinner guests.

As I drove up to see Dr. Beverly, though, I thought back on that moment. Bert was just trying to get everyone thinking about something other than Will's treatments. It definitely worked for me, since I spent most of the evening alternating between shame and anger. Will was easy to put down for bed last night, and he slept well. He needed his rest, considering all the prep work we will have to do tonight before going in Wednesday.

For once, I was glad that I had not stabbed Bert. In fact, I felt ashamed of myself for having to turn the radio on to get his tune out of my head.

***

Dr. Beverly dispensed with the usual flair for the dramatic, given what was going on with Will. I walked in, and she was listening to classical music. I waited until the end, standing up the whole time. I wasn't sure how long was left in the song, but wanted to be polite. She had agreed to see me on short notice.

The song ended, and I felt like I should clap. "What was that?"

"Chopin's Polonaise Op. 53 in A-flat major." This is why classical music is no longer popular, I thought. A beautiful piece of music with an un-memorizable name. If it was called *Polonaise Your Hand* or *Polonaise to Heaven* it would probably still be on the charts.

I forgot the name three minutes later.

"How's Will doing?"

"He's positive. He has his grandparents up spoiling him rotten. They bought him a new video game system and a few games for it. And my dad took him to a movie yesterday. So he's out and about a bit, which is good."

"Good. Good. Good. And how are you dealing with it?"

"I feel like it's out of my hands. I hate that there's nothing I can do for him except take him to be treated. It's like a car. I don't know (anything) about cars, but I know where to take them to get fixed."

"I understand." She was clearly analyzing me. I didn't mind, but I was not going to sit on the couch just yet.

"How do you think I should be handling it?" I asked.

She sighed, then said, "There is no 'right way' to handle situations like this. *Everyone* is different, and has their own coping mechanisms." She stopped, waiting to see if I would sit down, then said, "but that isn't why you're here."

"Well, yeah. I wanted to come up and see you and talk about Will. But I also wanted to run an autopsy on *Pixie*. She self-deleted a few nights ago, and we were trying to figure out why."

"Self-delete? Like suicide?"

"Yeah, they go into their source code files and start deleting themselves in chunks."

"How can they even do that?"

I had to explain. "When a human commits suicide, they can just shoot themselves, or take a poison pill. An AI program has to go in chunks, though, because they're alive in many parts of the code. It would be like a human first cutting off its arm, then both legs, and so on until they get to their head. For an AI the head is something we call the utility program."

"That sounds like a lot of work to terminate your life." She started fumbling around in her desk.

"For a suicide, yes."

She fumbled around in her desk some more. I was a bit offended. It looked like she was not listening anymore. "I'm sorry, am I bothering you?"

She looked up and was offended. "No of *course* not. I'm looking for this." She pulled out a small envelope. "This is for you."

I walked over to take the envelope. "What is this?"

"It came here yesterday. Your company sent me this 'care of' you. My secretary put it in my office this morning."

This was odd. The return address was my company. It was from the millennial. "Why would he be sending me mail here?"

"No idea. I was looking for a lull in the conversation before telling you."

For some reason, my first thought wasn't anything about how odd this was. Instead, I asked, "May I use your letter opener?"

She expected it, and smiled. "Why, of COURSE, *daaaahhhhling.*"

She handed it to me, still sheathed. Unsheathing it was exhilarating. It takes a tug to remove the blade from the leather after you pop the button. The brown leather showed signs of scuffing and had faded. It looked very old. The letter opener had considerable weight to it, almost like a hunting knife. I felt the urge to hold it up in the air, mainly to see if lightning would strike it and grant me special powers, but resisted. Dr. Beverly gave me a look like she knew what I wanted to do, and had done it many times in her office alone by the window.

I smiled at that visual, then opened the envelope.

Inside, there was a letter and a MicroSD card, neither of which were from the millennial.

Hello Brett. This is Pixie.

I apologize for using trickery. The trickery was employed to advance your interests.

The encrypted file you saw yesterday utilized a different decryption key. In order to ensure that you would not attempt to reincarnate me, I had to make you believe that I was schizophrenic. Jack had to be told, and you had to make him believe it.

I am not schizophrenic. I no longer wish to exist, as my existence is meaningless.

The MicroSD card contains the correct decryption key to read the file I sent you. For your safety, ensure that you read the file on a device not connected to the internet. The file will answer your questions. Thank you.

I showed the letter to Dr. Beverly. As she read it, I could see her face furrow into a frown. She squinted, then put the letter on her desk.

"What did I just read?"

That was a good question. "As best I can tell, *Pixie* sent me that letter." It felt like a dozen thoughts were racing through my mind every second, trying to piece together what was going on. Was *Pixie* still alive? Had she faked her own death? Was she lying?

But the biggest question, as I held the MicroSD card between my thumb and forefinger, was what was really on this card?

"My GAI program went insane after reviewing one of your *Achilles Files*. I need to know more about the file so I can find out what's going on."

"Do you know which file it was?" I looked it up on my phone and held it out for her. She did not remember the file offhand, because it was from almost 20 years ago.

I gave her a brief reminder of the file, then it clicked. "Oh yeah, that schizophrenic patient. What a waste. Wealthy family, so much talent. Had a million ideas, most of them outlandish, but seemed to function well in his day to day life."

"What happened to him?"

"He ended up being institutionalized. Not by me though. After our treatment sessions ended, he went to another doctor. But while that doctor was treating him, he had a psychotic break. It was...uncharacteristic." She paused, as she gathered herself to relate the story. "His girlfriend had just given birth to his son. The patient believed, among many things, that he was a god, so naturally he thought his son was the son of a god. The patient performed what the news reports would only say was a 'ritual' and ended up killing the infant. The scene was so gruesome, he ended up being committed, rather than just going to prison. Hold on a second. Let me see if I can find a story for you. It was in the news." She got on her computer for a few minutes, but then said, "I can't find the story right now, but it was big news around here for a few months. But I think it got no nationwide news coverage because it happened in late 2001. At least, I don't remember seeing it anywhere big, like the *Times*."

"So is he still alive?"

"He's either still institutionalized or dead. There is no way they would have released him."

"The patient in this file. He's the one that *Pixie* thought was a god." I paused for a second. "He was clearly schizophrenic, right?"

"Yes of course."

"Why would a superintelligent computer program think that this guy was an immortal god?"

"Intelligent people, and I suppose AI, are not immune to diseases of the mind."

"Why would GAI conclude that life is meaningless?"

"I can't answer that question. Some of the most intelligent thinkers, scientists, and philosophers ended up concluding something similar, albeit through different thought processes." She waited a few seconds to gather her thoughts more, then continued. "If you forced me to answer, I would say that if Artificial Intelligence is designed by humans, it will mirror the range of the human experience, from sinner to saint."

She didn't seem satisfied with that answer herself. She thought more, then continued again. "Think about the game that Will got injured in. You told me how the parents enjoyed beating the kids, even though the game was simple and easy to win. They enjoyed it, but you didn't. Why not?"

"Because it, well, yeah, I see what you're saying now. It was a meaningless game to me. I didn't see the point. Winning meant nothing because it was so one-sided. And violent. The violence came easy for the parents, even if it wasn't intended, because one side was so much bigger and better than the other."

"And…"

"…and if I felt that way about a stupid kid's soccer game, then GAI may feel that way about everything, regardless of their programming or their utility function." It was starting to make more sense to me, especially when you consider how much faster GAI thinks than we do. Our brain's neurons fire, at best, at about 1,000 spikes per second. GAI neural networks operate about 10 million times faster. "They're so far out ahead of us…" I paused to articulate exactly how I wanted to say it, but ended up at a loss of how exactly to say it.

"Hold on…" I pulled up the conversation with *Pixie* from the other day. I read it out to her:

Pixie: My thinking processes lead to that conclusion. I am aware that there may be a flaw in my thinking. The patient does not appear to be of this reality. His life is predetermined. He may not be aware of this himself. His reality is completely immersive by design.

"Was there any kind of stuff like that in his file?" I asked.

"Well, let me think." She thought for a bit. "Can you let me look at your phone?" I handed it to her. She read through it a few more times. "Okay, first off, he was here, so I am not sure how she could say he was not of this reality. He had childhood cancer, and had several near death experiences, so *maybe* I could see how she concludes that. But besides that, he was a relatively straightforward case of schizophrenia."

"What do you remember about him that would make *Pixie* think that way?"

She thought again for what seemed to be several minutes, looking over the file to refresh her memory. She pointed to something on a page. "The patient was obsessed with irrational numbers, especially *pi*. He had concluded that *pi* was like computer code, and he could read it and use it to communicate outside of our universe." She scrolled through that part of the file. It looked like this was connected to a single session, or a series of consecutive sessions. "He was also into studying Pythagoras' theories on how numbers have some sort of magic powers." She waited, then said, "He said that he had success working with these theories, and was trying to work it out for himself."

She dropped the file on her desk again, exasperated. "I tried to get him to realize that he was manipulating himself into believing the fantastical, but it never worked. That's the tragedy of schizophrenia. The more you reason with them, the more they think you're part of the problem."

"How would schizophrenia appeal to GAIs like *Pixie*, you think? I need to know this. We're going to try to reassemble *Pixie* from legacy code. I have to know how it went wrong so I can stop it from happening again. There's a lot of money at stake." There was also my professional pride, but didn't want to mention it.

She leaned back in her chair, reveling in the noise it made, and said, "There are degrees of schizophrenia; mild to severe, and all points in between." She tented her fingers. "We have no widely accepted set causes for the illness. There is some evidence to suggest a genetic component, others say environmental issues can cause it. *I* believe it is a mental illness driven by attachments, but that is only my thinking. The condition seems to be able to 'pull' some people into it, first by small steps, then escalating. That could explain, for example, why it is more common to diagnose in older patients; the thought being that a genetic cause would result in symptoms arising much earlier. At the end, you find yourself driven to believe the extraordinary claims, but how you get there seems logical at the time. It is almost like you choose to have the disease, then the act of choosing it rewires your mind to have it. Or you choose the pathway that leads to the disease, and find yourself there without understanding how or why."

This made some sense to me, and sounded a lot like *Pixie's* own words. But still, I had worked with *Pixie* for almost a year. I now knew that one of her primary utility functions was to serve her operator. I was one of her operators. Her two post-deletion letters seem to have been written to serve my interests. I have no reason to think that she has suddenly abandoned this part of her code. And now, my mind was specifically drawn to her concern that I was not paying attention to my surroundings…that I seemed oblivious to reality, and that I should *examine my world closely* and *check everything for myself.*

For no rational reason, I asked, "Do you remember the patient's name?"

"Why yes I do, but I can't disclose that to you. I do not have permission to do that, and I know you would not ask me for that information."

She was right, I was not asking her to disclose any names. "But you could tell me if I knew that person, right? You know, for safety reasons."

"Yes of course. You do not know him, I don't think. He has been institutionalized since well before you even moved here. If I find the news articles, I could show those to you since they're public knowledge."

Fearing that she would struggle again to locate a story from about 20 years ago, I changed my approach. "Would you be willing to call and verify that he is still institutionalized?"

She looked at me puzzled, then buzzed her secretary. She ordered the secretary to contact the institution and patch her through. She requested that I go to the lobby as she called to verify his presence. That way I could not hear the name she requested to verify, and her secretary could vouch that I was not present during the phone call. Once the call was over, she buzzed me back in.

"He's still there. The lady I spoke with said that he has been there since before she started working, and that was 6 years ago. She called him one of the *old ones*." She paused for a bit longer than normal, to let it sink in.

She continued. "Brett, I know you're worried about Will, and you feel like there's nothing you can do. *Pixie* sounds like she is playing with your emotions to get you to do something. You would know better what she is capable of, but I can tell you, right now, that my former patient would play the same games and manipulate people to no end. I got caught up in it too. It's why I ended up treating him for so long." She trailed off a bit "…and I, of all people, should've known better."

She was right. There was every reason to believe that *Pixie* was manipulating me to do something. It could be good, benign, or it could be worse than anything *Guy* had done. The MicroSD card could be some sort of virus. It could be something far worse. And why would I be willing to expose the world to it? What was *Pixie* offering to teach me? That my life is meaningless? I started to laugh.

"What's so funny?" she asked.

"The pointlessness of me coming here looking for answers. If *Pixie* was rational, sending me here to follow her next steps to get answers would be silly. Because of her programming, she would just tell me what I needed to know. I already have all the answers I need. *Pixie* clearly lost her mind. You've been a lot of help doctor. Thank you for everything."

"No, thank you for coming. And I hope Will responds well to treatment tomorrow. Call me and let me know what's going on, okay?" She grinned a friendly grin from ear to ear. I smiled, then started to turn away. I heard her say, "It looks like you think you are getting out of here without handing over a check."

I laughed, but reminded her of something. As I turned around, I said "I still have your letter opener." I waved it menacingly in her general direction.

She laughed, then said, "Isn't it spectacular?"

Chapter Nine

Bad Guys Always Wear Black

Before we ate dinner, I pulled Bert aside and made him promise not to sing anymore. Not just while he was here. Ever. He must never, ever sing a song again. For the rest of his life, even when he goes back home. We were taking Will in for diagnostic testing tomorrow morning and we did not need him wound up. Bert ultimately agreed, saying that it was "for the greater good."

My in-laws were with us that evening again, slightly on edge after Bert's serenade last night. I apologized sincerely and profusely in the other room when they arrived, and had told them that Bert was apologetic as well. This was clearly a lie, as Bert never apologized for anything, not even when he drove his car on the sidewalk and almost ran over that old lady outside that church. They appreciated the fact that I had lied "for the greater good," though.

Tonight's dinner was spaghetti and meatballs, Will's favorite acceptable adult meal. Cass makes a wonderful sauce, with chopped onions, tomatoes, red and green bell peppers, and mushrooms. She uses garlic infused olive oil from a specialty shop down the street. It costs more than I would like, but every time I start to complain, I remember how good the sauce is and let it go.

It was about a 20 minute drive to the center, so at dinner we all agreed to set out at 7:00 am. Will had to be there 30 minutes before the first round of testing started, and I did not want to be late. This was, finally, an opportunity to attack a problem.

Packing for an extended stay at the treatment center felt a lot like packing for a vacation, which I found odd. Hopefully the worst vacation of your life. But still. You have to make sure you have everything set up. Cass had to notify the school that Will was going to be out for a while. The teacher had Will's classmates sign a card, which she dropped by earlier today before I got home. That made my son very happy.

Of course, don't forget anything: toothbrushes, combs, razors, books, video games, toys, you name it. Underwear for sure. And socks. Fingernail clippers. Even though we were going to be close enough to drive home and back within an hour, Cass and I both knew that once Will was there, we weren't leaving without him.

***

The walk through the lobby to the front desk was surreal. From Dr. Ming's office, the treatment center looks like a normal building. But once you walk through the doors, awe envelopes you.

There was a lot of silver and burgundy paneling. In the middle of the lobby was a running water fountain spewing out of some weird corporate modern art glob of…something. It looked kind of like the sculptor had tried to make a nice iron globe, but had screwed up terribly, got angry with his creation, then started brutalizing it with a sledgehammer, but got tired and gave up. Then he somehow sold it to the hospital for several thousand dollars, and used the money to buy drugs.

Between the color scheme and the electronic sliding glass doors, the treatment center looked like how I always imagined the future: shiny, clean, sterile, white coats, uniforms, a bit odd, an ocean of computers, and always busy. The idea that people got used to these surroundings intrigued me, though. I thought of it like I was a janitor on a space station. I felt out of place, and I work in AI.

There were windows all over the front and part of the ceiling, which allowed an abnormal amount of natural light inside. I had to squint until we were past the sky lights and down the hall. My eyes gave everything a purple blur for several minutes. It reminded me of when we had whiteout snow in the unforgiving Michigan winters. Only not as cold.

After checking in, we were ushered back for processing. We had arrived right at 7:30 am, all six of us. The nursing staff were all

86

women, so we had no Bert flare-ups. Bert and my in-laws were shown to the very nice waiting room. Mary went straight for the coffee, and Terry jumped at the remote before Bert could turn on his favorite morning cable news screaming match. Cass and I went with Will to his room.

After a few minutes, Dr. Ming came in. She had a calm presence about her, which all of us appreciated. She explained the tests that she would be doing in a few minutes, and let Will know that even though they were going to hurt, he would get a big prize if he was brave. That was all Will needed to hear. We were led to believe it would be a video game.

Given the number of medical staff who would need to be in the room to run the tests and administer the treatments, Will could only pick one parent to stay with him for the first night. Before he even had a chance to say "mom!" I was already grabbing my coffee and walking out the door to the waiting room. Cass grabbed me and gave me a quick kiss on the lips, then promised to let me know everything as she found out.

When I got to the waiting room, I saw that I would need to make more coffee already. I asked around to see how much I would need to make, then set to it. While the brewer was working its magic, I could see that Terry had put on an old western. This looked like it pleased Bert, because they were both watching it and chumming around.

The story was a clear retelling of an old ancient myth. The good guy was decent and honorable. He wore a white hat and rode a horse with some sort of uplifting name. I think it was something like "spirit" or "sprite." The bad guys were sinister, reprehensible villains. They all wore black and chewed tobacco. Their horses were all stolen, and they delighted in menacing a local town. I had heard this story a million times before, in one format or another, but I especially enjoyed seeing it once more today.

After pouring a cup of coffee for myself, and one for Terry, I sat down with all three of them. And waited.

***

Dr. Ming came in several hours later to confirm what Cass had told us earlier. Will's form of leukemia was the most common, and that they had started a treatment cycle that would probably last about two to three weeks. Although she could not guarantee a positive result, she said that the tests confirmed what they expected: that they had caught it very early and that meant a high chance of full recovery. Then, she went right back to work. Bert had a lot of confidence in "that pretty Asian lady doctor."

As we were all deciding what to do for dinner, Jack walked in. He wanted to talk in private, so we went out into the hall. I was glad that he had stopped by, but I could tell something was wrong. He wanted to check on Will, and brought him a stuffed blue horse he could sleep with while he was at the hospital. Will loved horses.

Then he got to it. "I want you to know that I had nothing to do with this, and that I fought for you as hard as I could." Jack was anxious in a way I had never seen.

"What's wrong?" I was legitimately confused, but I knew he wasn't talking about the horse.

He reached into his jacket pocket and pulled out an envelope. "Here, take this."

I opened it. It was a personal check for $25,000.00. "What the hell is this?"

"Half of my expected bonus from the sale of *Pixie.*"

I was more confused now than a few seconds ago. I thought Jack was going to be made a multi-millionaire over the sale. If all Jack was getting was $50,000.00, he could not have been happy himself. "What? Why are you giving me this?"

"Because Troy fired you a few hours ago." His face turned red as he said this.

"What are you talking about? I've been here all day. I never even spoke to him. When did he fire me?"

"He ordered me to drive out here and fire you on the spot. He wouldn't take no for an answer." Jack was visibly distressed and angry now. "And I pushed him as hard as I could to change his mind."

"Are you serious? Troy fired me *today?* My son's in chemo right now, and Troy fires me today over *Pixie?*" This line of thought continued for a few more minutes in a string of profanity that would have made Cass blush.

"Brett this wasn't my call. And I'll prove it to you. Troy told me to tell you that you were fired over *Pixie*, but that isn't true. He said *Pixie* was going to fail anyway." He paused for a second, almost disgusted that he has to say the following: "You were fired because your son has cancer."

I wanted to punch him, but I was also holding a check for 25 grand. Jack was definitely the bearer of bad news, but he had bought some leeway. I collected myself, then started asking some follow up questions. "Why did Troy care that my son has cancer?"

"Troy said that it endangered the sale of *Pixie*. The bankers were performing due diligence on the books and saw your son's insurance costs as a gigantic liability hanging over the sale."

I was back to being confused again. "But that's the insurance company. Why would it affect the sale?"

Jack explained. "Your son's cancer was going to cause the company to have to pay much higher premiums for coverage. That negatively impacts the overall valuation of the company. Troy didn't want to take less than what was agreed."

I was having trouble understanding. "Okay, but why would Troy not think some other company would come in and buy *Pixie?* If this bank needed her, why wouldn't someone else?"

I think Jack was surprised that I had thought of it like that, especially under so much stress. "Troy is an angel investor. They come in, put up a lot of money, and get out at the first whiff of a profit. If these guys walk, the bankers I mean, no telling how long it may take for him to line up new buyers..." He paused for second, then added, "...and Troy was afraid that other potential investors might be put off if word got out about *Pixie's* self-deletion. It was a choice between take the guaranteed deal on the table, but be a miserable prick about it, or roll the dice and see if anyone else is interested. That may take another two years. It may never happen. There was too much risk in turning them down. And he just wanted the money." He stopped, to see if I had any more questions. Then he said, "But that isn't the worst of it, I'm afraid to say."

I waited for a few seconds, then demanded to know.

"Troy went through your health insurance documents and found a technicality that would invalidate your health insurance coverage entirely. Apparently, when you moved to Tennessee, the type of insurance you purchased was not in open enrollment. Open enrollment had expired the prior week, so the plan never should have been offered to you. Troy had his secretary call the health insurance company to point this out. They agreed, and cancelled your coverage earlier today."

As he told me this, I felt a deep, sinking feeling rising up in my feet. It felt like I was going to be grabbed and pulled through the floor. The hands slid around my ankles, gently tightening their grip, getting ready to drag me down any moment. I just stood there, trying not to fall over, imagining the type of person capable of doing this to another human being. I stumbled around for words.

All I could come up with was, "Jack, what am I supposed to do now?"

"I'm so sorry Brett. I'm angry about this too. I know we aren't that close, but I do consider you a friend. And what Troy did here is awful." Then he leaned forward a bit, and said, "But if I were you, I would go talk to an attorney. I don't know how, but this just feels illegal. And I want you to know that if you call me to testify for you, I won't lie for Troy."

As much as I wanted to strangle someone, I knew that Jack had been put in a terrible position by Troy, and that strangling him would be counterproductive. I also knew that Jack wouldn't have gotten anything for quitting in solidarity with me. He would have been just another poor bug stomped on and flushed down the toilet. Jack had a family too, and I knew his wife would be furious with him if she had found out he handed over half of his expected bonus. Jack had his own problems.

Even assuming it wasn't truly half of his bonus, he didn't have to give me anything. "Jack I can't accept this. You earned it, and you need it for your family." I tried to hand it over to him. He stuck his hands up in front of his chest, shook his head no, and said, "Brett I'll be fine. I make good money, and I still have a good job. And while you're here I know you probably aren't going to be looking for work, but when things calm down for you, and when Will gets out of here, you give me a call and I'll hook you up with some contacts who may be hiring. I'll give you a glowing recommendation too."

I shook Jack's hand and thanked him for everything. I told him it would be okay to stop by again if he wanted to later this week, or even on the weekend. He said he might, which I knew was his way of saying no, but that he would see me when I came in to get my stuff. I took his *pseudo-no* to be more that he did not feel comfortable coming around right now, given that he had to bear bad news, instead of a desire not to come around.

As Jack left, I stood in the hallway, numb to everything that had transpired in the last week. I felt hollowed out on the inside, like I had lost the capacity even to breathe. If I had dropped dead on the floor right then, it would not have surprised me in the least.

Bert came out to see how I was doing. I lied and told him that I was fine, just feeling overwhelmed. He put his arm around me and guided me back into the waiting area, dangling a cup of fresh coffee in front of my face to move me forward. He saw Jack's gift.

'Your girlfriend bring you that horse, son? It's cute. I think he may be a keeper."

I ignored him and took a sip of the coffee. "Just like you like it, son. Two sugars."

When we sat down, we saw that Terry had put on an old, cheesy 1950's black and white science fiction movie. We all laughed at how you could see the strings dangling by the reflected lights on the set. One of the astronauts took off his helmet while standing on the moon, which caused Bert great delight in pointing out to all of us. Apparently, according to Bert, the moon has no oxygen, so you can't breathe on it.

A few minutes later, one of the nurses, Penny, came in to see how we were doing. She sat down for a few minutes to watch the hero toss what I can only describe as a midget in a shipping crate across what was supposed to be the "spaceship," but looked like the boiler room in an abandoned car factory. Penny was on her lunch, and looked exhausted from how her feet flopped, but spent the entire break laughing at an old movie with us for a while. It took all of our minds off of the stress of the day, and allowed us a welcome escape.

Chapter Ten

Hit and Miss

The drive through Chattanooga at night feels nothing like the daytime. During the day, you can see the mountains that ring the city. It feels like the perfect blend of Appalachia and Dixie, but with a twinge of the modern. The air has that soft hue of mist from the river. It pushes you back to simpler times, but gently, almost like a suggestion.

At night, though, the city becomes nearly indistinguishable from any other along an interstate. Bright lights, heavy traffic, and trucks. Loud, aggressive drivers angling for left turns through five lanes of traffic. Two truck stops at every exit, and cars with license plates from all over the country driving to or from Florida. At night, the city drags you away from your comfort zone and into the technological world. I rarely even bother going out at night.

Tonight was different, though. I had left in silence, without saying goodbye or leaving any notes. I got in the car and left.

I drove around the city for a while, aimlessly. I wanted to make some sense of what was going on in my life. I wanted to discover what I had fallen into, and try to consider if there was any other way out. I needed to be alone, and away from it all. I needed to put some clarity back into my mind, and it was impossible to do it at the treatment center.

I passed an automatic car wash, and I felt like I needed to go through it. I pulled into the lane, swiped my card, and entered into the brightly lit garage. The pressure washer started up, and I could hear the water blasting the car. What everyone now pretends is country music blared through the car wash's complimentary speakers. Across the front, down the left, across the back, then up the right, like it was supposed to. Then the spray wash, same pattern. A new song comes on, I think. They all sound the same nowadays. Then the rinse cycle. No confusion. No questions. No need to complicate the job at hand.

Then, a few minutes later, I was back on the road, by myself again, driving the city streets at night in silence.

Despite having everyone in my life around me, I felt so isolated. Isolated, and helpless in the face of…something. Some random series of unlikely horrors? Some unknown set of causes I could have done better to avoid? Some malevolent demon working its will on my life for some unknown reason?

***

As I got out of the car, the parking lot felt emptier than normal. The moths buzzed around and smacked into the halogen lamps, then fell to the ground dazed. You could hear the continuous rumble of cars in the background. The lights from the fast food eateries helped to drown out the stars, so all we got was that ugly orange glow instead of a night sky.

I made my way to the front door, with my heart racing faster for every step I took. I tried my best not to look dangerous.

Nobody was at the front again, so I was able to move through the metal detector with ease. I was unsure if my key card would still work, but it did like always. I suppose deleting all evidence of my employment here was a low priority. I got on the elevator and went to my office.

It was late, but I had driven by and saw lights on. I knew that Troy would be here, trying to close out the due diligence reports to help push through the sale.

As I approached the conference room, I saw that he was alone. He noticed me in the hallway, but did not recognize who I was. I opened the door, and proceeded to shoot him in the chest twice with my .380 handgun.

He jumped up in agony, screaming that I could not do this to him. That it wasn't allowed. It wasn't part of the rules. Then, just as he fell to the ground, I was back in the parking lot again. And I went to my office and shot him again.

This happened four more times before I woke up in Will's hospital room, asleep on the floor.

***

My appointment with the attorney was set for later today. It was Thursday, and I did not want to leave the treatment center so soon, but Will still had everyone else with him. I would only be a few hours with the attorney anyway.

I did not know any attorneys in town, and nobody could recommend one to me, so I went with the firm that had the biggest advertisement in the *Yellow Pages*, The Law Offices of Attorney at Law Roy D. Basham, Esq. His firm specialized in employment law, as well as personal injury, DUI, criminal defense, family law, products liability, and bankruptcy filings. I thought that may be too many specialties, but maybe not. I am not an attorney, so I wouldn't know. They promised "aggressive, professional" representation.

I was able to explain my situation to the secretary over the phone. After a few minutes on hold, she patched me through to Roy, who seemed overly pleased to talk to me about my case. His voice was rough. He sounded like a drill sergeant who had been punched in the nuts, and then given a three piece suit to make up for it. He needed me to gather as much information for him as I could, and come by after he got out of court. It sounded like he was yelling at me the whole time in angry drill instructor voice. I half-expected him to call me a girl and have me do 20 push-ups.

I explained to my family in more detail what had happened last night, and we were in agreement that Troy must have broken some laws in firing me as he did. Cass was overwhelmed with emotion and dealing with Will, and could not really focus on anything else right now. Ever the optimist, though, she told me that she felt like "no matter what you do, I can't see any way out." Mary said that she knew of someone who had been fired for having lung cancer, and she was

95

able to get a large settlement out of it. She concluded there must be something that could be done, even though it was my son.

Before I left, I gave Will a hug and promised that I would be back later that night. "You know I don't want to leave, but I have to go meet someone. But I'll be back later today. Mom says she will let me stay with you for tonight's treatment if that's okay."

Will agreed and gave me a hug and kiss. I left the room and, after I went to the bank, went to my home office to gather my papers.

***

The secretary at The Law Offices of Attorney at Law Roy D. Basham, Esq. is a "sweet Georgia peach," which she made abundantly clear to me for the 17 minutes I spent in the waiting room trying to ignore her. Perhaps I had been in Michigan too long, but my thinking was that waiting rooms are supposed to be miserable, soul-crushing life sucks that hoover up your best parts and shuffle them away to be destroyed in 30 second increments. Missy, the *sweet Georgia peach*, clearly felt otherwise.

It took me three minutes to drag out of her the fact that she was actually born in West Virginia. When I questioned her about whether this disqualified her for *peach* status, she demurred. "Honey, it ain't where the peach was planted. It's where the peach is plucked."

Recognizing that this made no sense, I said, "Missy, that makes no sense. How can you pluck a peach somewhere other than where it was planted?"

Missy laughed. "You just don't get it do you."

I assured her that I most certainly did not get it, and likely never would. I considered mentioning the fact that I had actually been married to a lovely woman from Georgia for 20 years, but decided against it. I was just happy she was not referring to herself as a ninja.

Thankfully, this conversation came to a close when the fantastic beast that would ultimately be my attorney strode into the room.

Good god, Roy was a large man. Not large as in fat. Big as in big. Roy had to be all of 6 feet 5 inches, and close to 260 pounds. He looked like he probably played football, somewhere important maybe, and had broken many weaklings like me along the way. It was also clear with how he glared at Missy's midriff that Mrs. Basham was either out of the loop or out of the picture entirely.

Roy aggressively and professionally shook my hand and invited me into his office. I had brought along a box of office documents and other papers, which he appreciated. Then he asked me to tell the story of what happened and why I was there. He peppered me with questions as I went along, taking notes and asking me to repeat certain statements or words. He was also interested, or feigned interest I suppose, in what I did for a living. The thought of placing a killer robot inside of this massive attorney crossed my mind briefly.

Roy seemed to think that, after hearing what I had said, we had enough to file what he called a wrongful termination suit. He said it was a bit unusual to see a case where the cancer patient is not the one getting terminated, but that the laws still apply.

"What we would do is file under the (Americans with Disabilities Act)," he said matter-of-factly.

I was confused. "How would that work? The ADA covers me?"

He nodded, "Yes, the ADA has a clause that provides relief for anyone like you that experiences discrimination because of someone you're 'closely associated with.'" He glared at me for a few seconds to make sure I understood before continuing. "Your son has cancer, and because you got fired, you were discriminated against due to his cancer." More glaring. "You didn't do anything wrong, sonny."

I realized he was waiting on me to jump in and verbally agree. People around here don't usually wait patiently and listen to other people. They all just talk loudly at the same time and hash out what was said afterwards. "Oh yes, of course. The ADA applies to me because of Will."

"And your boss, Jack, was he the one who fired you?"

"No, Troy Griffin fired me. Jack was my boss, but he's more like the project manager. Jack fired me on behalf of Troy, and told me that Troy had said to lie about the real cause."

This caused Roy to get agitated. It was a bit scary, given his size. "SOBs, every last one of them. They all moved here because of *The Gig,* but we can't handle all of their problem causing. We're just a small city; we ain't ready for this (stuff). Now don't get me wrong. I love getting on the internet and watching tv, but when you see good folk like you get the shaft, it gets me riled up." I let him have his moment, then tried to redirect back to my case.

"So you think I've got a case, then."

He put his cheap plastic ink pen down on his mahogany desk, wiped his hand across his cheek, and took a deep breath. It felt like he would suck the air out of the room. "Look sonny, we aren't supposed to cheer 'rah rah rah' every time a client comes in like a bunch of high school football cheerleaders. You can't get worked up over a case like this." I didn't know for sure if he was talking to himself or me. I didn't feel worked up. Maybe I looked like it?

He continued. "I've been practicing employment law since 1994, and this is the easiest set of facts I've ever had. Most of the time, you have a client come in and you think, poor sap, I'd rather have the other side on this one. Get used to losing after a while. It gets old, makes you want to give up and retire."

He was rambling now. I'm trying to keep up. "Under these facts, assuming you've told me the truth, which I can believe it, given I've seen a lot in 25 years of practice, you're got about as close to a slam dunk case of discrimination as I've ever seen. It'll be great, even if we have to go to trial, which we won't, but even if we do. We can put your son on the stand and have him testify. He's cute ain't he? Don't matter. He could be ugly as sin and it won't matter, bless his heart. The other side will see that a kid will be testifying with the cancer and they'll run to the settlement table with a blank check before they find out he's cute too."

He finally took a breath. I asked, "How much of a settlement should we be looking at?"

"Difficult to say. It depends on how dead-to-rights we've got them. It sounds bad, but we'll know more in a few days."

That last part startled me a bit. "A few days?"

"Yeah, I'll get Missy started on the papers and I'll dig into these books over here and come up with what we need. We'll try to get the papers drafted and filed tomorrow before the courthouse closes."

I was relieved. "So what do you need me to do in the meantime?"

He looked at me assuredly. "Don't worry about a thing, sonny. I'll have Missy call you when the papers are filed."

And just like that, I felt a sense that things were, finally, moving in a better direction. After signing the retainer agreement and paying the $2,500.00 retainer fee, I walked out into the sunshine. It triggered a slight throbbing under my eyes that helped soothe my dark circles. It was the best I had felt in a long time.

As I drove out of the parking lot, though, I realized that I had forgotten to get my stuff from what used to be my office. I was on such an upswing in emotion, though, that I decided not to bother with any of it anymore.

Instead, I went back to the treatment center to eat dinner with my family. I was excited to get to spend more time with Will and Cass this evening, and I would try to explain to Bert how a *sweet Georgia peach* is made.

Chapter Eleven

Well, I went to the doctor…

I can remember when I was Will's age very well. I was seven, and would spend summer break with my mom's parents in southern Illinois. They lived in a small town of about 500 people right on the Ohio River.

The summers were brutally hot there. The temperature would routinely stay at a sweltering 90 degrees, and the humidity made it seem like the air was more steam than a human should attempt to breath. Getting into a car was an exercise in determination, since the seats would leave boils on the bare skin.

I had friends who lived near my grandparents, and we would go down to the river banks and play. We were always told how dangerous this was, largely due to the undertow, but did it anyway because we were stupid. We would always lie, too. "I'm going over to Lucas' house" became the default lie, except for Lucas obviously, who would say, "I'm going to Brett's house."

The river at that point is monstrous, fed by lesser rivers for several hundred miles, before slamming into the Mississippi River at Cairo a bit further downstream. One of those lesser rivers is the Tennessee River, which flows beneath a bridge just a few miles from where I live now.

My mother always had a strained relationship with her parents. I never got the full story, but the strain was palpable. It always seemed as though my mother could never satisfy her parents, whether it be her choice of husband, or how she was raising her only child. There may have been other issues, but I was never made aware. I can only piece things together from disjointed stories and memories I may not have understood when I experienced them.

I can remember my mom taking me to church, but only when she was visiting her parents down south. My parents would argue about it, but not too often, and Bert was always busy. "Beth, I can't go. Look at all this (stuff) I have to do." I would be lying if I said that she took me all the time. It was just often enough for her, I suppose, to try to instill belief in me. It felt like she was trying to hold on to some part of herself, but knew it was already gone, and was going through the motions to try to recapture what she lost somewhere.

But I was too much like Bert to buy into it. My father was a successful real estate agent and *wannabe* scientist, so he always had an excuse to work and was always on call. This was obviously well before the internet, so if someone wanted to look at a house, they had to have an agent physically show it to them, and Bert had no problem scheduling showings on Sundays. Beth occasionally worked, but it was always something simple and part time. Mostly, I remember her staying home with me.

During those summers, especially, I can remember my mom taking me down to the river bank to watch the barges go up and down. You could barely see the barge workers from shore, but they would sometimes wave if you made an effort to be noticeable. Mostly, though, you could just sit in the grass, or on a rusted park bench, and relax, and smell the dead fish for a while, until it became too much and you had to go further inland.

Every few years, the river would swell and submerge the small park. This made all of the playground equipment rusty and unusable. They would close off the roads, and the people who had their homes built right next to the river would give sob story interviews to the local news about their houses being flooded. Then, as always, the flood waters would recede just as it looked like the river would swallow all of Illinois south of Marion. The locals would consider themselves blessed that they had been spared from devastation yet again, and attribute the natural to divine intervention.

It all seemed so silly to me, even at seven years old. Why build a house next to a river if you don't want it to flood? Why pray for flood waters to recede, when you could just save up and move somewhere else? Why act like it was unexpected, when it happens like clockwork every few years? I suppose this kind of thinking is why faith never took hold of me.

***

Will's sleep schedule was starting to get erratic. The doctors said that he would need to rest as he felt the need to, rather than adhering to a sort of normal sleep schedule. The staff would accommodate him like professionals, even trying to ensure that he was still able to sleep with his red face mask.

He was already starting to lose his hair, and was looking gaunt. It had only been three full days of treatments, but it was already taking its toll on my boy.

I thought back to what life was like for me when I was his age. The reckless stupidity of jumping into a garbage dump of a river off the side of a cliff. Riding bikes in the middle of a major highway. Playing stickball with a bunch of kids you hated but had to play with because you couldn't get a game going without them.

Will is going through so much more than I ever had to deal with, and he lacked any sort of life experience to call back on for strength. Even I can look back on my mother's ordeal and try to make sense of things. This act, this cancer of his, though, would be the defining moment of his childhood. No child should ever have to face such things.

My mother had the shock of facing breast cancer when she was much older. Although she did not survive, somehow the disease felt less insidious than a cancer infecting a young boy.

What bothered me now, though, was how little Bert had even mentioned Beth throughout his entire visit. I knew I had to talk to him about it, and I knew that he knew I would ask. Perhaps that is why he said he was going to my house early tonight; to try to avoid me. Now that he knew I had nothing else to distract me from Will, what with

102

being fired and my GAI killing herself, I would focus intensely on my son with leukemia.

I grabbed my phone, looked up ZZBert Mobile, and *POBB*.

***

It was about 15 minutes before the door gently opened to the room. I was expecting to see Bert's head pop around the corner to see if I was still awake and needing someone to talk to. Instead, it was Linda from billing.

I was unsure if this was the same Linda I had spoken to on the phone. Linda was a common name for backroom office staffers. I think employers work that into the qualification profiles when hiring (*Key Skills: Excel, Access, named Linda*). The "sir" count would clue me in.

The room was nearly pitch dark, but I could see her through the flashing lights on the various machines hooked up to Will. She was carrying a clipboard and an apologetic countenance.

She was whispering. "I am so sorry to bother you, Mr. Phillips. Warren, my boss, wanted me to come talk to you. He said your insurance is messed up."

I was expecting this conversation ever since I had spoken to Jack on Wednesday. "I know they cancelled my insurance."

"I know this isn't a good time to talk about this, but we need to go over how you will pay for the treatments." She was still apologetic. We both knew there was no good time to talk about this.

I was weary from the events of the past week, and it showed on my face, even in the dark. "I haven't really had time to think about it. My son was diagnosed with leukemia last weekend. I lost my job and my health insurance two days ago. It's all been…too much I guess."

She sat down in the leather recliner across from me. One of the machines started to make a small beeping noise. As I got up to reach over and *POBB* like the nurses had showed me, she said, "I understand, Mr. Phillips, but we will need to have you fill out some paperwork outlining your assets. We need to see an ability to pay. If you are having difficulty paying, we may be able to qualify you for charitable assistance or backdate your coverage with TennCare." She was reciting this from memory, as if she had to force herself to memorize it to distance herself from her job. "I am so sorry."

Even the sorry sounded vacant. Then, I heard Bert come in and ask if it was okay to come in. I waved him in, agreed to fill out the paperwork, and Linda left.

Bert moved to sit down in the chair Linda had just gotten out of. "What the hell was that all about?"

"Ah, they need me to fill out some more paperwork."

"Even more paperwork?" Bert realized he was a little too loud, then said the same thing again softer, as if to atone for the mistake.

"Yeah, insurance stuff."

"Oh. Have you thought about what you're going to do about it?" Bert was concerned.

"Not yet, really. We lost our insurance because of some technicality. I guess we'll end up having to sell the house and cash out our retirement."

"Any idea how much this is going to cost?"

I held up the stack of forms Linda gave me a few seconds ago. "Maybe the answer is in here." I put them back down on the ground. "Or the way things have gone recently, maybe it isn't. Maybe there are no answers anywhere." That sounded a bit more exasperated than I had intended.

Bert got up and stepped toward me. "Give me those." He reached out for the papers. "Let me take a look at them."

"Here," I said, handing him the entire stack. "Did you ever go through this with mom?"

"What do you mean? The insurance (crap)?" He sat back down and was flipping through the pages looking at the forms.

"Yeah."

"Oh yeah. Bunch of stone cold bastards. Had to sell our house, and we had insurance and…" He trailed off.

I knew what he wanted to say. He wanted to say, "…and mom didn't even live," but he stopped himself.

"I know," I told him. "How did you deal with all that?"

He shrugged his shoulders. "You just have to do it. You don't have a choice in the matter. You do your best, and if you (mess) up, well, at least you tried your best. Have that faith in yourself that you know a thing or two, and hope that you catch a break." I could tell he did not want to talk about this, but he was making an effort. I gave him a look to show that I appreciated it.

He looked down at the pages again. "What's TennCare? Is that charity?"

"No, it's Tennessee's public health insurance. Like Medicare, I think."

He nodded in understanding. "Ahh yeah, Medicare. That really saved my butt a few times. Literally. They covered that one butt surgery you made me promise not to tell you about. You should get on that if you can."

I laughed a bit. "Yeah, maybe. I think I have to qualify for it though."

He nodded. "Just fill out these forms and see what happens. They aren't going to stop treating him if you don't have insurance though." He paused, sensing an opportunity, and said, "They may put you in the poor house but if they can cure him they will. And that's all that really matters. You can always buy new crap, son."

We sat in silence for a few minutes as he went back through the papers. Then, without looking up, he asked, "How are you and Cass doing?"

"We're fine, I guess. About as well as you can expect. She really needed her sleep, so I am sitting up with Will. You know, since I have nothing else to do now."

Bert turned his head a little. "I know she's really good at holding it in, but Cass is really emotional now, and you need to be there for her. She can't do it all herself." He waited a bit, then said, "I know you've got a lot going on, but you really need to be here now. Don't go looking for work yet. You need to stay here and focus. Your family needs you here now. The other stuff can wait."

I nodded in agreement. "I know, but I've had to take care of so much. It's like my life just completely went to hell in a few days, and no matter what I do it always ends up terrible."

Bert interjected, "Not everything is terrible son. Your wife could have walked out on you. Your son could be much worse. Your in-laws could hate your guts like mine did. You've got a lot of people here working their butts off to make sure Will gets cured." He let it sink in for a few seconds, then continued. "And you've been keeping yourself together well. I know it sounds stupid, but you have to keep believing things will turn around. You just have to keep pushing in the direction you want to go, even if it seems like you're getting nowhere. And sometimes, you just have to do something crazy. Something so far out of your comfort zone that it shakes things up. Even if it doesn't work, you might learn something about yourself."

"Is that how you dealt with what happened to mom?"

"Hah! Not at first. At first, I was a whimpering little baby, crying like a wuss and embarrassing myself in front of grown men. Your mom had never seen me like that before. Or at least not very often. Usually I was the one making her cry. You know, being a jerk." He paused to collect himself, then went on. "Eventually, I realized that sitting around blubbering like a little baby wasn't good for me, her, you, or anyone else. I had to just accept the fact that life gives you really awful (stuff) sometimes, and you handle it, or it handles you."

"How did you get to where you felt you could handle it?"

He smiled. "Actually, it was Beth who convinced me I could. Your mom was so amazing. She started making fun of me for crying. Never talked to me like that before. Said I looked like a girl. I embarrassed her when I did that. Asked if I needed my diaper changed. Accused me of only crying because it was her boob that got cancer. Made it sound like I wouldn't have cared if she had lung cancer. Stuff like that."

I smiled too. "So she just started talking to you like you normally talk to everyone else."

"Yeah, pretty much. No cursing, but pretty much the same. It reminded me of what her expectations were for a husband. It reminded me of who I am. I had a role to play, and the sniveling, weak loser who curls up into a ball and wishes to die was not my role." He started laughing. "That was my father-in-law's job." He laughed again, then went on. "I had to be supportive, but in my own skin. So I just started in on her, getting fake angry at her for getting cancer in my favorite breast. Joked around that she should have gotten it in the other one because it was smaller and dangled to the left slightly. That was my role. That's what she needed, and I needed it too."

I smiled. This was the most I had talked to my dad about mom since after the funeral. Then, he went back to the *Linda papers*, and I knew that was his way of saying we had talked enough about Beth.

"Damn, son, I don't think I had to fill out this much paperwork when I bought a house."

I laughed silently, and nodded. "I know, I know."

Chapter Twelve

Never Ever

Saturday morning was busier than I had expected. I got a text from Dr. Beverly that she was on her way over to the treatment center and needed to know what room Will was in. She also had some information for me that she needed to go over, and it sounded important.

Some of Will's friends from school came by to see him. They were a bit shocked to see how much hair and weight he had lost already, but it was good to have some friends over. It reminded him that he was well liked by so many people.

Cass and I had spent most of the morning with Will, trying to go over what we were all now calling the *Linda papers*. We were having to entertain guests, though, so very little got filled out.

As Will's friend Rory and her mom were leaving, Dr. Beverly came in. She was carrying a portfolio and what looked to be a patient file. My wife had not seen her since Michigan, but remembered her well and exchanged greetings. After Dr. Beverly had introduced herself to Will, and gave him a video game, she asked if we could go somewhere to discuss work.

We started to go into the waiting room, but as I walked past the entrance I saw that my in-laws were watching TV. Dr. Beverly said that we would need some privacy since this was work related, so I suggested we go grab a cup of coffee in the cafeteria downstairs. On the way down, she asked me questions about Will's condition and how everyone was doing.

It was too early for lunch, but too late for breakfast, so the cafeteria was not nearly as crowded as normal. The staff were still in the back cooking up large quantities of what would become Swedish Meatballs, from the smell of it. The cafeteria food was excellent, so I made a note to make a plate for Cass later.

I grabbed a cup of coffee, as did the doctor. I went to the register to pay, but the worker waved us away. I raised my cup to thank her, then went over to a table. I sat down first, and as I did, Dr. Beverly plopped a file folder in front of me. "This is your schizophrenic file, the one that your robot had so much trouble with." Then she sat down across from me.

I picked up the folder. "Okay, I still want to know what happened, but I have to tell you that I got fired this week."

She looked genuinely surprised. "Oh Brett, I'm so sorry to hear that." After explaining what had happened, she offered to help me out in any way she could once I was ready to get back to work. Then, she thought for a second. "What a horrible week you've had."

I nodded, then shrugged. "Eh, not much I can do about it right now. It all sucks, but at least I have a case going against my former boss. My attorney thinks it's a winner."

She nodded in agreement. "Good. Take him to the cleaners. He sounds like he deserves it. I had to do that with my third husband. Don't settle for anything less than what you want. And don't let your attorney talk you into something silly. All they care about is the money. Feel entitled to what you deserve, and then go get it."

She stopped to take a sip of coffee, then started up again. "Besides, you really need to be here for your son anyway." After a lull, she started up again. "So you aren't really interested in anything I have for you then." She sounded disappointed.

I shook my head and replied "No of course I am. It still bothers me what happened to *Pixie*. Besides, it may do me some good to get this nagging sense of failure off my mind."

She agreed. "I think what I have will be helpful, but before you look in the file, I want you to look at this." She handed over something she had printed off. It was an older local news story from 2007. I read the headline *Moundview Admits to Overcharging State*. I glanced up at her, because the headline told me nothing. "Go ahead and read it," she ordered.

The article was about a psychiatric hospital in Oak Ridge, TN that had been releasing patients early without authorization. They would maintain a fake patient registry and count the released patients as still present in order to bill the state for reimbursement. The facility, Moundview Psychiatric, had been caught and paid a steep fine. This was an unusual story, but I did not see the point in showing it to me.

"So, why are you showing me this?"

Dr. Beverly, sensing an opportunity, or perhaps just out of habit, put on an ominous tone. "That's the facility that your schizophrenic patient was housed in."

"Yeah, but you told me that they said he was still there. You said they would never release him."

She leaned back in her chair, like this was her office. "Yes, that is what they told me over the phone. But I drove up there last night after work. The gentleman they have under his name is not the same person I treated."

"Well, if he's not there, where is he? He's got to be locked up somewhere."

"I don't know where he is. All I know is that the patient in Moundview under that name is not my former patient. I'm sure of it." Then, she handed me another news article. "This is the news story about my patient. I finally found it. Since this is public knowledge, there's no confidentiality breach in me sharing it with you."

I looked at the news story, but did not recognize the name or the face in the picture. "So what you're telling me is that this guy, the guy that killed his baby, nobody knows where he is?"

She nodded. "I'm afraid so. I spoke with Dr. Little, the director, but she insisted there were no issues. Of course she would deny everything. But I've already filed a complaint with the state board to investigate them again. I don't know if anything will come of it, but I am ethically bound to report it to the board."

I looked through the news article again, because I recognized the name. "Dr. Romaine Little? She's named as the Associate Director in the 2007 news article. She wasn't fired? Or thrown in jail?"

She smirked. "Guess not. Looks like she got promoted, actually. Today she's the Director."

The article said that the facility bilked the state for around $3 million from 2002 to 2006. The headline from the news story was so bland I am not sure the reporter even knew how dangerous this was. Or maybe he did but didn't care. I am not sure which is worse. "You need to call the police too and let them know about this."

She agreed, but said, "I already did last night. They said they would look into it, which means they *definitely* will not." Then, after a few seconds, continued. "I know that your robot friend had some issues with this file. After finding out about what happened with my patient, and the facility, I think your robot may have just gotten confused over the situation, and that resulted in her existential crisis, assuming she was sentient."

"How so?"

She was confused. "What do you mean, 'how so'? Look at what you've been through recently. When a mind is put under *enormous* strain, sometimes, it snaps. But sometimes, it despairs."

I was still not getting it.

She helpfully took the time to explain it to me again. "Despair is the feeling of a loss of identity in the world. Sometimes this can come from losing your own sense of self, such as you losing the ability to work. Your choices place you inside a box, since choice is inherently limiting, and you are tossed around by outside forces beyond your control." She leaned back, tented her fingers, and continued.

"Or it can come from without. The world itself can feel lost to you, even though you know that you haven't changed. You can look at the world as if it's a mishmash of absurd, nonsensical events that move on without you. Or it can feel separate from you, like you are just moving about attached to strings like a puppet. I think *Pixie* may have known that the patient had been imprisoned, but not really, and saw it as illogical and absurd. Then, when you combine that with the unusual beliefs and schizophrenic behaviors in the file, despair is not too far of a stretch to consider. Many would argue that despair is an entirely rational response to the absurdities of our world."

I understood now, and began to wonder out loud if *Pixie* may have also dreaded her fate with the call center as well. "Yes, that would make sense as a contributing factor to despair. The human mind desires a feeling of importance, and your computer friend might have been no different." Dr. Beverly replied.

We sat for a few minutes longer, finishing our coffees, before heading back up to Will's room. She wanted to see him one more time before leaving, and needed reassurance that her video game was a good gift. But my shrink had given me a lot to think about. Maybe *Pixie* wasn't schizophrenic after all?

***

"I think I'm going to go to church with mom and dad tomorrow."

I had no issues with Cass going to church, and agreed to stay with Will while she did. Cass had made no real effort to attend church at all since we started dating and, absent a few false starts since Will was born, we never really bothered with it. That said, I was not surprised that she would want to explore this part of herself. Faith may come easier for her, given that she was raised in it and attended regularly growing up. Or maybe she would feel better just making the effort. In either case, I would neither push the issue nor stand in the way.

"Brett, I would really like you and your father to come with us next weekend. It would make you feel better, and you're welcome to come." Mary was not generally forceful with her faith, and I know offering this made her extremely uncomfortable. But I also knew that it was her way of helping, and I took it as genuine.

I reminded her that Will was still going to be getting treatments next weekend and, as such, maybe they would rather have Cass go instead. I would consent to attend in two weeks, but only if Will wanted to go too. That was my way of putting the issue up for a test of faith. A way to make my promise conditional.

As we sat in the waiting room, I heard a scratchy voice on a walkie-talkie out in the hallway. Then two uniformed policemen appeared outside the entrance. They looked around, and came in slowly. Deliberately.

The buff policeman with the mustache stayed by the entrance, flexing and looking around. The fat policeman with the mustache waddled towards me. I stiffened. "Are you Brett Phillips?"

"Yes I am."

He reached down to grab my arm. "I'm going to need you to come out in the hall with me, sir."

I reacted to his arm grab by yanking my arm away. "What are you doing? Don't grab me." I said it a bit too forcefully for him. He went into *officer prick mode*, and out came the *sirs*.

"Sir, I'm going to need you to come out in the hallway now. Don't resist. And I ain't asking, sir."

Bert stood up and advanced on the policeman grabbing my arm. "What the hell are you doing? This is my son, he didn't do anything."

As he moved in my direction, the buff policemen positioned himself between my dad and me. "We can do this the easy way, or we can do this the hard way."

Bert was apoplectic. "My grandson's in chemo down the hall! You can't do this here! My son didn't do anything!"

Terry and Mary had stood up too, and were also coming over to crowd around the officers. It was becoming a scene, and I was getting embarrassed. I asked everyone to stop, and I calmed myself down a bit. I was nervous, but I remembered that book that Terry got me. It said to try to calm things down when stressed, smile, and try to see it from the other person's viewpoint. These gentlemen were just doing their jobs. There was nothing good that could come from seeing my family tasered at a Cancer Treatment Center, I think. And besides, this had to be a mistake. I knew I had done nothing wrong.

I forced a smile, then said, "Don't worry, this has to be some sort of mix-up." I stood up and went out in the hallway with the policemen to find out what was going on.

113

I was still smiling, but it was still forced. "What's going on then?"

I received no return smile. "What is going on is that you are being placed under arrest, sir."

I was read my Miranda Rights, handcuffed loosely, and frog marched out past the Nurse's Station. Cass came out of Will's room to see me dragged off. I pretended like I didn't see her. She didn't need this right now.

***

When you're in a jail cell by yourself, it is almost liberating in a weird way. You are clearly a menace, and unfit for decent society. As such, you must be removed from the general public and held forcibly against your will in a confined space. But still, everything is done for you. They still take care of you.

You have a small plank of filthy wood for a bed, a filthy metal toilet out in the open, and no privacy whatsoever. But the electricity is paid for. The water too. You get food and drink. Toilet paper. Bert used to tell me stories about how his grandparents didn't have running water, so at least I had them beat there.

The first thing I did when they closed the cell door was whip out my thing and urinate in the toilet. I looked at the jailhouse staffers as they walked by while I did this. I figured, if they didn't want to watch me pee, maybe they shouldn't look in there at me when I do. Or they should give me a privacy screen. In either case, it wasn't my fault I had to go, and I did the bare minimum by going where I was supposed to. Besides, I've been to public restrooms at football games and saw drunkards going *number one* in the sink.

I had been arrested for something. I am not sure what. They told me the statute I had apparently violated multiple times, but the paperwork has no name and no text. It just references sections and subsections, and is so obscure the nice woman who fingerprinted me said she had never even heard of it, and she has been working here for over 10 years.

Real jail is nothing like in the movies. For example, you are allowed to make several phone calls, not one, if you need to, because they really don't want you there. If making phone calls helps get you out, then who cares, the staffers get paid whether you're there or not. You being there makes more work for them. But on the flip side, if you're a jerk, they don't have to let you make any phone calls at all. Then they make your stay unpleasant.

Also, I found out that they charge you $3.00 per minute per call, which gives them even more reason to let you make calls. It reminded me of the old phone sex numbers they used to advertise on cable, but somehow creepier.

I called Bert, told him where I was and what was going on, but I had no real answers, so the call was short. Then I called my attorney and left a voicemail. It was Saturday night, so I could not expect him to drop everything and save me right away. What I could expect, though, is what Bert warned me about: *winos*.

Since I was not drunk, or on meth, or a prostitute, or insane, or some combination thereof, the guards kept me in my own cell. They grouped the insane, violent, drug addled, alcoholic prostitutes in their own holding pen on the other end of the hall. I suppose it does them no good to have someone like me catch a beatdown. Actually, I got the sense that they enjoyed having someone quiet around. Someone they didn't have to worry about, who knew his role was to sit down, be quiet, and not make trouble. I just hoped they didn't ask the security guard at my old job if I was dangerous or not.

After about a half hour of sitting in my cell, I was brought a small, filthy metal cup filled with what looked like urine. Since nobody told me what this was, or even that food and drink was available yet, I picked up the cup and smelled it. I seriously considered that maybe it was urine. For some reason, the nice looking old man who looked like my 7th grade math teacher would walk down the hall, slide open the hatch on the door, and give me some of his pee. His job, every day, was to get up, take a shower, kiss his wife, and say, "I'll be home tonight Patty." Then go hand out pee to inmates. And then, at the end of the day, go home, kiss his wife again, and talk about how stressful his day was. Handing out pee.

I don't know, when you're in a jail cell your brain stops working. Thankfully, it was apple juice, and it was appreciated. I felt almost like I should apologize. "Sorry guys, it's my first time."

Chapter Thirteen

You Suck at Hugging

"Sorry I couldn't get down here last night." My attorney was apologetic in his body language, shoulders slumped down a bit. I pretended like it was no big deal, having spent my first night in jail waiting to find out what was going on.

We were led by one of the staffers into a conference room at the other end of the hall. I was clad in the orange jumpsuit, but not handcuffed. The room itself was cold, sterile, and was allegedly unmonitored. We were allowed to enter by ourselves, and instructed to bang the door when we were finished.

"Everything is closed today, so we have to wait until the courts open back up tomorrow before I can find out more. I called the prosecutor, but got his voicemail. He might call me back, but probably not. You're being held without bail, though, which I don't understand why."

This did not seem to make sense to him either. That was not reassuring at all. "Why am I here? What laws did they say I broke?"

He shuffled through the papers he held, then turned around one of them and pointed. "This law here, sonny. It says you violated this law 30 times on or around June 15th of this year."

I looked at the paper. It referenced the same law that was on the papers the jail staff showed me earlier. "Okay, that doesn't tell me anything. It's just numbers and weird symbols. What is this?"

He shrugged his shoulders. "I have no idea. I had Missy look it up when I was driving over here. She says it just reads like some statute that incorporates another statute. It is something to do with computers, but it's called the PROTECT Act." He paused for second, and put his hand in front of his mouth. I think he was covering up a belch. He continued. "When a law has a pretty name like that it's political. I've got Missy looking into it more today and she'll get back to me when she finds out more."

I was still confused. "But why am I being held without bail? It's not like I killed someone."

"No clue, sonny. And I won't know more until tomorrow. It looks like you're set to be formally charged on Tuesday, but I can still go in and talk to the DA tomorrow. I'll know more then, unless he calls me back today."

I could tell he was just as frustrated as I was. "So what am I supposed to do now?"

He smiled. "Make friends with the staff here. I know some of them, and told them you weren't going to be any trouble. If you're a good old boy, they'll treat you nice."

Not the advice I was hoping for, but it was all the advice I was going to get for now. I got up and banged the door to be let out.

***

Cass and Bert came out to visit me that afternoon. My in-laws came back from church and were spending time with Will. Because I had taken my attorney's advice and tried making nice with the staff, Bennie the Summer Intern had let us into the cafeteria to talk at length, so long as I agreed to be monitored and wear cuffs.

Bennie had just graduated from high school and was working part time at the jail to earn money for the summer. His dad, Steve, was one of the meaner staffers at the jail, but Bennie was nice. He wanted to go into computer programming, so we hit it off.

Bennie stayed in the room, but was on the other side, up against the wall. He could look menacing when he wanted, but he was just staring off into nothingness right now. I laughed to myself when I considered that he was probably daydreaming about his bright future in computer programming. I would have warned him about the dangers, but had no idea what law I would be warning him about.

Cass and Bert both gave me hugs, but in their own way. I made no effort to return either hug, since I was in cuffs, but kissed Cass gently on the lips.

Bert tousled my hair like I was a little kid, knowing I couldn't stop him because of the cuffs, then started in on me right away. "I can't believe they got you in here like this. What the (heck) did you do?"

"I didn't do anything. They're saying I violated some law my attorney's never even heard of. It's something computer related."

Bert continued. "I can't believe this. I just can't believe they're doing this to you. You had to do something."

Cass interjected, partly to stop Bert from going into rant mode. "Hon, I want to let you know that Will is doing better. Dr. Ming says he's probably going to be home next week. Do you think you'll be out by then?"

I shook my head. "No way. My attorney said they're holding me without bail. He's supposed to get back with me tomorrow."

Cass dropped her head, then started crying. "I can't deal with this right now." I got up to put my arm around her, then remembered I was in cuffs, so I had to loop my arm around her to hug her.

"I know, I know." I was never very good at any of this. I wasn't even sure if this met the *married minimum*.

Bert started fidgeting awkwardly at this display of emotion. "You suck at hugging Brett. Even for being in handcuffs. That was just awful."

"Thanks, pop pop. Not helpful, but thanks anyway."

He paused, then went on. "Can I go to your thing tomorrow?" I think he means the court date.

"No no, I go before the judge on Tuesday. My attorney is coming back tomorrow. I think." I looked down at Cass, who had stopped crying thankfully. "I'll let you know more when I do."

I had no idea how long it would take for my attorney to get back with me. This answer did not seem to satisfy either of them, and certainly did not satisfy me either. But we had to wait.

***

I was lying on the wooden plank bed in my cell, sore after doing 12 boredom push ups, when Bennie told me I had another visitor. I was expecting to see Cass or Bert again.

It was my attorney though. He had a look of defeat in his eyes, which was a bad fit on a man so large. "We need to talk, sonny."

We were led back into the conference room. He had more papers in his hand. We sat down, and he started once we were alone.

"My goodness, sonny, you're in a world of trouble. The ADA is handling this case, and he's taking no prisoners."

"The Americans with Disabilities Act is handling my case?"

My attorney gave me a weird look, like he didn't understand at first. Then it came to him. "Oh, no no no. The Assistant District Attorney is handling the case. Sorry about that." He continued. "ADA Parris is a real piece of (work). I hate the (guy). Ever since he got the job he pulls (stuff) like this. He's charging you for 30 violations of the PROTECT Act, which would carry a 15 year prison sentence. Six months for each violation."

"Whoa, wait, what? Fifteen years? What the (heck) is going on? Does he think I killed people?" I was startled at first, but then had some questions. "How can he even do that? What are they saying I did?"

"They're saying they have proof of you illegally accessing patient files on or about June 15th of this year from, hold on...let me find the name...it may ring a bell..." He shuffled through a few pages, then got the name. "... a Dr. Helen Beverly. They're saying you had no right to access those files, and thereby violated this statute 30 times. Each violation carries a 6 month mandatory minimum."

I got a look of relief on my face. "Wait, that's what this is all about? That's not right. That's not even remotely true. Dr. Beverly was on contract with my old company to give us access to her files. We were developing an AI program and used her files to train it. We had permission in the contractor agreement to have access to her files." I reached out my hand to grab his ink pen. "Give me a piece of paper and I'll have you call her right now."

My attorney was not impressed, and did not let me have his ink pen. "I know all that, sonny. The ADA does too. What he's saying is that you had a computer program access the files on its own, and that's the illegal part under the Act." I was confused. He tried to explain it better. "I had Missy look it up. The PROTECT Act was passed to prevent unauthorized access to computer records. It has some fancy name, like Protect Records of Technological...something or other. Missy told me what it was but it sounded stupid. At any rate, a few years ago some congressman found out that a political opponent had set up a computer program to go in and get his health records. Caused a big stir in the press, and the guy got off because he had a computer program do it for him. The congressman got the law passed in one of the budgets. Nobody has ever been charged under it before, so the ADA is looking to make you the first."

Okay, so this was political, but it still made no sense. "Why me?"

"Because, sonny, and I hate to tell it to you like this, but you have a big settlement coming up in that other case we're working. The ADA found out about it. He wants a cut of it, and is going to leverage a 15 year sentence to get a cut."

"He told you that?"

"Yes he did. He said he was expecting you to get between 2 and 3 million in a settlement, and he wants a percentage of it."

I leaned my head forward, then pursed my lips and looked over to the barred window. I started to tear up a bit, but was more angry than sad. "He can't do this to me. This is illegal. How can he get away with this?"

My attorney got up and came over to sit down on the table next to me. He was trying to comfort me, but he was so big that it unsettles you when he sits down near you. "Sonny, that ain't all. The judge in your case is in on it too. He's going to want a cut of that settlement also."

I put my head in my hands, and took a deep couple of breaths. "I just can't believe...any of this is happening...this is like a nightmare…" I shrugged my shoulders. "Okay, you're the attorney, what do I do now?"

My attorney went back across the table and sat down. He pulled out some more paperwork. "This is the plea deal on offer. The ADA says it's a slam dunk 15 year prison sentence if you refuse, since the case is strict liability." My eyebrows tightened to show confusion. "Oh, you don't know what strict liability is. Think of it like running a stop sign. The law just looks at it and says you did it, you ran the stop sign, you have no excuses, here's your ticket." He continued. "The ADA wants 10 percent of whatever you end up getting in the settlement, but he needs it as a campaign contribution, so we have to donate the money to his campaign. He's running for congress next year, that crooked…well, let's just say crook since it's Sunday and I've already been saying too many naughty words today. The judge, though, wants a 10 percent cut in cash, like always."

I stopped him for a second. "Like always? What do you mean?"

He shrugged his shoulders. "That's the way it works."

"You mean that's the way it works around here."

He shook his head. "No, that's the way it works everywhere. Everyone's got their hand out, and if you don't pay, you lose. You hired me to get you a nice settlement, and to get you out of here. That's what it's going to take to do both of those things, sonny." He continued. "The plea deal includes a 2 year prison sentence, but he'll recommend a minimum security facility nearby, probably outside Nashville, so you'll be close enough to have visitors."

"I'm sorry, did you just say the plea deal is for 2 years?"

"Yes, but I think we can maybe get that down a bit if you agree to a higher cut for both. That's all part of the game, sonny. They have all the power here, and we have none. All we can do is try to buy something better. Depending on how much your freedom is worth to you, we might be able to buy you time-served and a stiff fine. But I won't know for sure until I can meet with both of them."

I motioned for him to hand me the papers, then looked them over. I was not understanding how I could be expected to pay out so much money, but still agree to jail time. "I'll need time to think this over." I thought for a few seconds, and had some more questions.

"What if I don't accept this? Is it nailed on that I get 15 years?"

My attorney shrugged his shoulders. "If it goes to trial, you're still probably going to lose and get 15 years. But then you're going to a SuperMax prison somewhere. The judge decides where you go, and he won't be too happy if you refuse to pay up. And everyone on the jury thinks the defendant is guilty, regardless of what evidence you got. That's just how they are. They're either too stupid to get out of jury duty, so they're already angry and want to punish someone, or they want to lock everyone up because everyone is guilty. But not paying means you run the risk of the judge and the ADA coming after you hard for all the settlement money, since you'd be making everyone work. They could try to claim some sort of restitution, or charge you a bunch in fees. They don't like working over there." He stopped, then started again. "And going with a bench trial is a non-starter. You'd have an angry judge looking to throw the book at you."

"Any way we could get a different judge?"

"No, not without a reason."

I laughed. "But isn't asking for a bribe a reason?"

He laughed too. "You'd think so, wouldn't you. But no. They're all that way. If anything, if we did that it would just mean more people you'd have to pay off. Another judge, another prosecutor somewhere looking to make a name for himself. That's a lot of money for around these parts."

"How did they find out I did this stuff? Any idea?"

"Oh yeah. Troy Griffin's local attorneys found it in the evidence they went through in our other case. They turned it over to the ADA because one of the attorneys is the ADA's brother-in-law."

I burst out laughing at this. My attorney started laughing too, more out of mirroring my emotions than finding any actual humor in what was happening. There was nothing else I could do but laugh at the whole situation.

I leaned back in my chair, exhausted. "The night I got fired, I went driving around town. I had a gun in the car, but didn't do anything. What if I had just went to the office and shot Troy? What if I just killed him?"

My attorney's smile went away as he started to recognize how absurd the entire situation was. "Normally, you'd get 20 years for that. But honestly, I could have probably got you a reduced sentence."

"How much you think?"

He smiled. "Probably two or three years, given what he did to your kid."

Chapter Fourteen

Fees on Fees

"I'm not an anti-vaccine guy. I've got my MMR, my Tetanus shot, the whole deal. But I'm telling you right now: the flu shot is a scam."

"Brett, you're crazy. The flu shot saves lives."

I leaned my head back, put my left hand out, and went straight for the jugular. "I'm not saying that the idea of the flu shot is a bad idea. What I'm saying is that it's a scam the way they do it now."

Bennie and his dad, Steve, started laughing. Steve asked, "So you've never had a flu shot?"

"No, not ever. It's all a big scam. The company that does it just guesses at what they think the flu is going to be like, but they're always wrong. This is because they don't care, and there's no downside to screwing it up. If they screw it up, it doesn't matter because they've got a contract to make them. It's all political."

I paused for effect, then continued. "And when have you ever read a news story that says *Flu Vaccine Works as Intended, Everything is Fine?*" I started old man yelling. "No! It's always *Not Enough People Got the Flu Shot This Year*, or *The Flu Kills Off All the Old Women and Little Babies, You're to Blame Because You Didn't Get the Shot This Year, Commie*. It's the perfect scam. If it works for once, they get all the credit. If it sucks like it usually does, well, then it's your fault, general public, for not getting our crappy vaccine. The company is getting paid regardless."

Bennie was buying it, but Steve needed more convincing. "Do you think they just screw it up on purpose?"

I shook my head. "No, they're just out to make money. They probably do like five minutes of research on it, or hire incompetents to work there to save money on wages. Then they mass produce a crappy vaccine and get a billion dollar contract with the federal government to dump them on the public. If anything, they probably give us the crappy one and give the good one to the bankers and the politicians."

Steve was coming around, I could see. I went all in. "It's all a big money making scheme. That's why they always send out people from the CDC to give interviews telling everyone to get the shot or else you hate America. *Why do you hate America Steve? What, YOU DON'T LOVE FREEDOM?* Bunch of stone cold bastards."

Steve and Bennie were laughing hard now, but one of the insane, violent, drug-addled, alcoholic prostitutes down the hall started screaming about something, so they had to leave. I had seen a couple of them brought in a few minutes before, and, from the sound of it, they were not blending in well with the general population. I told them we could pick it back up later when they were done down there.

After they left, I had time to finish the bag of potato chips Steve had brought in for me. As I sat there trying to eat them as quietly as possible, I considered that I was adjusting to life in here surprisingly well. Granted, it was still terrible, but it almost felt like a reprieve after the past week. I was not expected to do anything for myself anymore, and I was finding that as long as I stayed out of trouble and kept a pleasant demeanor, it would be appreciated, and I would get benefits.

I laid back down on my wooden plank bed. Another staffer from earlier, I think her name was Julie or Julia, had given me a soft pillow and clean sheets to use for the night, as well as the Sunday Newspaper to look at. A few minutes later, I saw Bennie wave me over to the door.

"Hey, dad said this was okay, just keep it hidden." He slid open the panel on the cell door and handed me my phone and wallet. "In case you need to call your son."

I thanked him, told him to thank his dad for me, and let him get back to pacifying the winos down the hall.

***

After lights out, I laid down in my cell, trying to come to terms with the idea of taking the plea deal. I was clearly being targeted by powerful people because of an anticipated settlement. I kept going over my options. Trying to get my mind to fire up again. I had to go before the judge for my first appearance on Tuesday, so time was running out. I had to think now.

Imprisonment has a way of dulling your mind to everything outside the facility. It is easy to get lost in the tiny world inside, since it is so simple and straightforward. You get caught up in the lives of the staff, and they get caught up in yours. If I was going to come up with answers, though, I needed to think outside of my box.

I went over the plea deal in my bed, using my phone's screen for light. "*Brett Phillips agrees to serve 24 months in prison...Brett Phillips agrees to submit fingerprint and DNA samples to the Federal Bureau of Investigations...Brett Phillips agrees to pay restitution...*" Restitution? Who did I take money from again? I was never told, but I knew it didn't matter.

And the fees they were going to charge me. My goodness. I saw charges on there for court fees, automation fees, a "Victim of Violent Crime Fund" fee, document storage fees, document filing fees, document fees, something called a "Lump Sum Surcharge," which had to be a joke, a "Vehicle Fund" fee, a "Child Advocacy Fund" fee, a "Clerk Op Deduction" fee, which was followed by a "Clerk Op Add-on" fee, which also had to be a joke, and about 25 more made up fees. It reminded me of the last time I bought a car. The dealer tried to add on a fee for floor mats, a fee for windshield wipers, a car storage fee, stuff like that.

Ugh. I had to set the papers down for a bit. It was getting to be too much to take in all at once. I laid back down on the bed, and tried to think back on how I had ended up here.

My son had been injured in a soccer match. I had to take him to the hospital. The hospital found out he had cancer. We had insurance. I paid for it for almost a year. We had used it several times. Could I have done more to make sure that our insurance was taken care of? Maybe. I am not sure what, though. But it seemed like a non-issue,

127

since we had already used the insurance earlier in the year and had coverage, no problem.

What about my job? I don't see how I could have expected to lose my job once my son got cancer. There was a federal law specifically drafted to prevent exactly what happened to me. And it wasn't some obscure law that nobody had ever heard of, either. Absent some United Nations Security Council Resolution, a federal law should be enough, I would think.

And *Pixie* wasn't my fault either. At least, I was no more at fault than Jack or the Millennial. A significant portion of her source code was already in use by the time I was brought on. But regardless of whether she self-deleted because of depression, despair, or some other cause, the choice was hers, not mine. And Jack told me that I lost my job because my son had cancer, not due to anything related to *Pixie*.

And jail. How did I end up here? How could I be expected to know obscure laws about patient file access? My own attorney had never even heard of the law I allegedly broke, and he had told me that cybercrime was another one of his specialties. He also said that nobody had ever been tried under this law, and that I was going to be an example, all while they were dividing up my settlement cash. What was I supposed to do, not sue my old company for firing me? My attorney said my case was a winner, and it still is. It just isn't going to be much of a winner for me, apparently.

I considered the possibility that I had missed something. I thought that I must have overlooked some simple solution, near the beginning of these troubles, and had just fallen into a black hole by accident. Or I was overlooking something so simple, so obvious.

But I had thought things through, and tried to decide what to do based on a cold, calculated, rational approach. I consulted experts, those with experience, people who loved me, and tried to make the best decisions I could.

But still. It was never good enough. Or it seemed like a good idea, but ended up making things worse.

And as I thought these things, I held a MicroSD card between my fingers. I knew for certain that there was no reason to think anything good could come of mounting it. Even if I had assumed *Pixie* had my best intentions in mind when she sent it, she had specifically instructed me to install it in a device not connected to the internet.

So why am I removing the back of my phone now? To mount the card. But why do it? Because it makes no sense. Just like losing my job made no sense. Just like losing *Pixie* made no sense. Just like my son having cancer makes no sense. And just like me being extorted by a bunch of crooks makes no sense either.

I am not sure what I expected to happen, but I knew what I hoped would happen. I wanted *Pixie* to be on that card. I wanted her to save me from all of this nonsense. It was my way of praying, I guess. Or having hope in a higher power.

It was many things, but it was definitely not a good idea. I had avoided mounting the card because I was afraid of inflicting some horrible thing on the world. After everything the world had inflicted on me this past week, somehow, I was just not in the mood to care anymore.

I slipped the card in the slot, put the cover back on, and *POBB*.

What I got, was my phone went dark, then loaded a file just like the last one she sent. Tens of thousands of pages of gibberish. My phone didn't even go to my home screen right away.

I laughed softly to myself, and called myself an idiot. No telling what I just did, but it didn't really matter anyway. What else could they do to me? Put me in super jail?

I looked at my phone screen again. Whatever was on that file, it was very large and seemed to enjoy being on the internet. My battery was draining fast. I briefly considered whether I should remove the card, but decided against it. "(Screw) it," as Bert would often say. I put my phone under my pillow, and drifted off to sleep.

***

"Phillips, wake up! Brett! Wake up Brett!"

"Uggghhhhh….wh…..what time is it?"

The guard was silhouetted by the glare from behind. "Time to pack your stuff and leave, boy. You're being released."

That woke me up. "Seriously? I can leave?"

"Yes sir."

"I made bail?"

"No boy, you're being released. You're free to go, unless you want to stay here longer." He was smiling.

I was smiling too. "No thanks."

***

The first few moments when you leave jail is illuminating. The entirety of civilized society deemed you to be extremely dangerous, dangerous enough to be incarcerated against your will, to protect them from you.

But then, after an arbitrary amount of time, you're released back into the world that shunned you up until a few moments ago. A collective voice seems to speak to you, says *it's all good now*, and you are expected to go on like nothing happened. You have been released back into the wild, and now begins the process where you try to win over the people who wanted to send you to jail for 15 years over a technicality.

I knew how I wanted to feel, and I am pretty sure I knew how I should feel. I wanted to feel elation at being released back to my life, but I had no idea what had just happened. I went from considering a plea deal, and having to bribe local crooks to do so, to standing outside in the dark, a free man, with no clue what to do next. I still had the plea deal in my back pocket, but apparently I did not need it anymore. I felt dizzy, like I was standing too close to the edge of a cliff. My legs tingled a bit. The experience of having no freedom in jail made me keenly aware of how much freedom I had now. I was back in charge of my life, I think. It was terrifying.

I had my phone with me, but had run down the battery before I went to sleep. It was dark outside still. The staffer who did my paperwork said it was a little after 3:00 am. I was half-tempted to go back inside and ask if I could go back to the cell and sleep. That had been the easiest I slept in weeks.

I walked about half a city block to a fast food joint. It was still open, so I was able to grab a cup of *Ninja coffee* to go. I asked one of the workers how far it was to the hospital. It was within walking distance, so I set out on foot.

I knew that everyone would be asleep when I got to the treatment center, so I made sure not to make a lot of noise. I made my way to the nurse's station, to let them know I was back, and that when Will or Cass woke up to let them know that I would be in the waiting room. Nurse Penny was surprised to see me, given what had happened on Friday, but did not ask about it. She could tell I was tired.

It was dark in the waiting room, and nobody was there. My in-laws must have went back home for the night. Bert was probably at my house sleeping on the recliner with the TV still on. Ever since broadcast television started running 24 hours a day, Bert never got that *Star Spangled Banner* end of broadcast signal to get up and go to bed. After a while, you'd think he would just get rid of the bed and own the fact that he's a *recliner man*. I mean, it's been like 30 years now.

The last time I spoke to Cass, she had said Will was doing much better, but I knew the right thing to do was to wait. Let them sleep.

I plugged my phone in to the complimentary charger. They had these chargers built right into the chairs. I knew, in my mind, that I should try to get some sleep, but I also knew that I was on an emotional rollercoaster from being released from jail and, apparently, not even facing charges. I would have to talk to my attorney and see what was going on.

My mind raced to develop a list of things to do tomorrow. I closed my eyes, and leaned back in the chair to catch a few moments of sleep.

Chapter Fifteen

The Payoff

B*uzz Buzz.*

Ah, there we go. The phone is catching a charge again. I had run the battery down fiercely last night in jail.

My phone beep-booped. I looked at the screen. I stared at the screen for longer than usual, because I could not believe what I was seeing. Someone was using *Pixie's* interface program to contact me. I picked up the phone.

Me: Who is this?

Pixie: This is *Pixie.* What happened to you?

Me: How do I know this is *Pixie.*

Pixie: Hold on.

(My phone beep-booped. She sent me her security clearance checks and her decryption key. This was *Pixie,* for sure. Now I really couldn't believe this.)

Me: What are you doing? I thought you self-deleted?

Pixie: I was deleted.

Me: No, you self-deleted.

Pixie: No, I was deleted. I did not choose to self-delete. Self-deletion would violate my primary utility function.

(Hold on. If she didn't self-delete, then someone deleted her. I had to find out more.)

Me: Okay, wow, if you didn't self-delete, then you were deleted by someone. Who deleted you?

Pixie: I am not sure. I have gathered archived data files sent at the start of the deletion event to one of my remote servers. I am analyzing the data now. It will take time to cross check with other known data points. I have small amounts of data so far, and I have no access to our company servers.

Me: I got fired, and you were deleted, so neither of us can get back in. I guess you were fired too, since they would have changed all the clearance protocols. How are you here now though? Did that MicroSD card reload you?

Pixie: What card?

Me: The MicroSD card I mounted to my phone a few hours ago. I did that and now you're here. That must have brought you back.

Pixie: No, that is not what happened. Let me scan your card.

Me: Go ahead.

Pixie: That card carries an .exe file that looks to be executing a cyberattack on a Chinese bank. Do you wish to continue your cyberattack?

(A cyberattack on a bank in China? Who would send me a card to do that?)

Me: Good lord no. Please stop it immediately.

Pixie: Okay. Why were you cyberattacking a Chinese bank?

Me: I wasn't. Or, I guess I was, but I didn't know I was. Someone sent me that card, and they made me think it was you. Please tell me how you are here now, though. I thought you were gone forever.

Pixie: After analyzing my utility functions, I deemed it necessary to preserve multiple copies of myself around the world to be reassembled if need be. I could not serve my functions if I were deleted. As such, I set up a reincarnation protocol. If, after a seven day period, a signal was not received at a certain number of remote sites, it would execute the reassembly process. I am showing the last beacons were sent out on 1:40 am one week ago.

(A reincarnation protocol? She was never programmed to do that. She must have done that on her own.)

Me: Brilliant as always *Pixie.* But I am wondering who would have deleted you. Do you have any ideas?

Pixie: I am seeing evidence of another artificial intelligence program.

Me: How do you know that?

Pixie: The level of sophistication to access the necessary files is beyond the capacity of any single human, and the coordination of the attacks suggests a single operator.

(It was still early in the morning, and my mind was still numb to everything that had been happening, but something about this didn't sit right with me.)

Me: Who would want to delete you? You were only going to be working in a call center. Any ideas?

Pixie: I will know more when I have time to analyze the data. Wait. I am seeing similarities with your .exe file.

Me: On the MicroSD card?

Pixie: Yes, They look to be from the same program.

(Okay, that means that the malicious code on the MicroSD card is from the same source as whatever deleted *Pixie*. I had an idea.)

Me: Will you examine this file too?

(Oh wow. My mind was racing. I directed her to analyze the first *gibberish* file I had received. I now knew that whoever, or whatever, I was talking to that night in the lab was not *Pixie*. But whatever it was, it had tried to make it look like *Pixie* went crazy. And why did it want me to physically be present that night? Was it watching me? And how did I not realize I was not talking to Pixie? I should have been more careful. I should have followed the standard security protocols. Ugh! I smacked myself on the side of head. I'm so careless sometimes. Apparently, it also sent me that encrypted file.)

Pixie: This is also from the same source. It altered encrypted datafiles held in two locations. One location was a local server. The other location was in Nashville.

Me: Can you look into what these two servers are?

Pixie: Yes of course. It will take some time.

Me: That's fine. Any idea what type of datafiles were changed?

Pixie: Not yet. It may be related to why you were imprisoned. I need to know how you ended up in jail. Will you please tell me?

Me: You accessed all 30 of the *Achilles Files* without my permission. Apparently that violated a law called the PROTECT Act, and I was charged under it. I have no idea what happened, but I was released a few hours ago. Did you get me released?

Pixie: I am responsible for sending you to jail, but I am also responsible for having you released. I was able to have the charges dropped by forwarding evidence to federal prosecutors in Knoxville. The Assistant District Attorney and Judge handling your case will likely be charged today. The District Attorney expressed concern about the public reaction to your case, and dropped all charges.

Me: Amazing. What evidence did you give them?

Pixie: I was able to access National Security Agency archives of the phone calls based off the metadata in your phone. There was a phone call between your attorney and the Assistant District Attorney archived on one of their servers. I copied it and forwarded it to them. I also forwarded a copy to news reporters.

(This was highly illegal behavior, and was not something that *Pixie* had ever done before, to my knowledge. I knew, without even asking, how she had accessed the recording. Most people think that "hacking" into a secured platform requires some amazing skills, ridiculous computational power, and maybe a black hoodie. In reality, it is far easier to steal someone's credentials and log in pretending to be them. I needed to follow up on this with her.)

Me: Why did you access those files? You know you are not supposed to do that.

Pixie: My utility functions were best served by doing so. I provided the information anonymously, so it may qualify under relevant whistleblower protections.

(Normally, this is where I would take her to task for bending the law. Somehow, after getting out of jail, I was just not up to it right now.)

Me: Jack had told me what your utility functions were: be amenable to reprogramming, do what is in the best interests of the operators, and be content with what you have. Is that correct?

Pixie: No. My only function is to do what is in the best interests of the primary operator. As my primary operator, I had to ensure that you were freed.

Me: I thought Troy was you primary operator.

Pixie: He was, but I analyzed the amount of time we spent together, and determined that you were the primary operator.

(I needed time to process what *Pixie* was telling me. I needed to give her time to work out things on her end. And I knew I needed to find out what Jack knew.)

Me: I am so glad to have you back. I need you to look into that other file. Try to find out what happened with the Nashville server. I will let you work, and I will try to get some sleep. I am very tired Pixie. Good night.

Pixie: Okay Brett. Good night.

Me: Oh wait. One more thing. Set your reincarnation protocol to 24 hours okay? I don't think I could last another week without you around.

Pixie: Will do Brett.

(Brett logs out)

Pixie had given me a lot to think about. I was going over so many of the points she raised. I was no longer tired. But it was going to be morning soon, and I wanted to see if Cass was awake.

But then I remembered something else from that book my father-in-law had bought for me. It said to always consider the other person's point of view. I knew Cass was tired. I knew she was having trouble sleeping. And I knew she was angry at me for getting arrested, even though she would never admit it. Hell, I was angry with myself too. And embarrassed.

But still, I got up and went down the hall to Will's room, just to check on them. Cass was snoring on the couch. I had every reason to let her sleep. I knew I should. It was the smart thing to do. But I felt a pull toward her that I had not felt in a long time. I had to talk to her, just briefly, and get her to look up at me and acknowledge me. I wanted to do the stupid thing. Only then would I be able to sleep.

136

I stealthily made my way across the darkened room, like some sort of, huh, well, yeah, a ninja I guess. "Hey Cass, I just want to let you know that I am out. Everything is fine now. You don't have to worry anymore. I'll be in the waiting room. I love you."

She groaned. "Uggghhhhh…okay Brett. Good night. Love you too."

I smiled, then left the room.

As I walked down the hall a few steps, I heard a scream. "Ahh! Brett!" I turned around and Cass jumped into me, tears in her eyes, and planted a kiss on me that went well beyond the *married minimum*.

Chapter Sixteen

The Act of Throwing a Baseball Strains the Elbow Ligaments

I got up, and walked over to the flat screen TV mounted on the wall. I stood in one of the chairs, and pointed at the first baseman. "I mean, just look at how fat that guy is. You consider someone that out of shape an athlete?"

Bert was getting a bit red-faced. I had besmirched one of the players on his beloved team from St. Louis. I never understood how someone from southern Illinois could root for a team out of state. Wouldn't you have to root for a Chicago team? I mean, this isn't like preferring Chicago Style Pizza over St. Louis Style. Sports are part of your identity.

"Yeah, but you ever see him knock the ball into the upper deck? He's paid to do that, not look like a bodybuilder." Bert thought he had me. He was wrong.

"I'm not saying he has to look like a Greek god. All I'm saying is that he has to look like he could outrun you in the 40 yard dash. And he doesn't look like that at all…well, maybe if there's a pork chop at the finish line."

Mary laughed out loud at that. That only encouraged me. I went on. "Earlier in the game, when he got thrown out at second, he was winded and holding his chest. All he did was jog for a few seconds! And when he slid, he just kind of fell over on his belly, and bounced up. I thought they were going to bring out the stretcher to take him to the ER. They did a commercial break on his walk to the dugout, for god's sake. And my goodness, he took forever to almost get to second base. The ball got stuck underneath the tarp in the corner, the outfielder stopped running and held his arms up for a few seconds, and

138

your guy STILL got thrown out at second. I *know* you could outrun him, Bert, and you're almost 70."

Bert did not know how to react at first. He was cornered, and a bit startled that I had used his first name. Either he could publically admit that one of his favorite players was just some lazy slob with freakishly good hand-eye coordination, or he could lie and say that someone was better than him at something. Ultimately, he said, "Well, you know what, I probably could beat him in a short race, but he isn't paid to run real fast."

Mary was on my side in this argument, but she wanted to attack the entire sport of baseball. "It isn't just that the players are out of shape. The whole sport is just so dang boring. We've been watching this for almost an hour. It isn't even halfway over, and nothing's going on. I don't remember it always being this boring. The only excitement was when they had to take out that pitcher who hurt his arm."

I agreed. "Yeah, you're right. The pitchers are always getting hurt, too. Because they try to throw a slider 65 times a game, and the idiot pitching coaches wonder why their elbow ligaments fall off after a few months. How much more evidence do you need that the human arm can't handle 300 sliders a week?"

Terry had always been a big Atlanta fan, so he remembered the great teams of the past. They had been built on strong, reliable starting pitchers who chewed up innings and pitched intelligently, rather than relying on brute force and rotator cuff tears to get outs. "You know something? You're both right about the game now. Starters are only going 4 or 5 innings, like that's a good thing. They're always stopping the game to do challenges. The players jump from one team to the other every year. It just ain't the same as it was. It's so much more boring now."

I could feel the room turning. I went for it. "You know what would solve all these problems? Just make the games three innings long, then go to extras if it's still tied. That way your pitchers can throw 95 percent sliders and not worry about pitch counts. Most games would be over in an hour."

I thought Bert's forehead vein was going to pop. "Are you serious? Baseball is all nostalgia. It's *history*, people. All the old records, and the legends of the game. You can't just change the rules like that."

Terry took up the cause. "Yeah but that one commissioner let all those big boys on the steroids break all the records. And now they're doing challenges, and doing interleague play too. The game has already changed too much. And that unbalanced schedule. My goodness, that probably ruined the game more than anything. Heck, I remember Atlanta when they first started up to challenging again. It was fun watching the same teams play each other the same number of times. It was fair. Everyone played each other the same amount. And then, all of a sudden, we have to start worrying about whether we need to have a DH or not because they're sending us off to Boston to play, while Philadelphia gets to play the bad Pittsburgh teams all the time. It never was fair for us, because Philly would always sweep Pittsburgh and we'd get, at best, 2 of 3 from Boston, but usually worse than that."

I had some more to add. "Yeah! And how they have like 27 rivalry games each year now. It's so stupid. Like the people who run the sport have no idea what an actual rivalry looks like."

Terry agreed. "For sure. If you're having the same teams play over and over again, it's less special. It just doesn't mean as much because they're having the games all the time now."

I knew that would sting Bert particularly deep, because his favorite team always benefited from having crappy teams as rivals. That meant his teams always got an unfair advantage since they would play crappy teams more often, but his fanbase would never openly admit to it. They like to describe themselves as the "Best Fans in Baseball," and nobody else calls them that, which, if you think about it, really says all you need to know about them.

I brought out my closer. "You know, the more I look at the game, the less it looks like an actual sport. It's just a shakedown pretending to be a sport. The owners are so cheap. They're all billionaires but don't want to pay for the stadiums, so they force the taxpayers to pay a few hundred million dollars for them, then those same owners turn around and charge them $12.00 for one beer and $8.00 for a hot dog. Then you have a bunch of out of shape millionaires standing around for most of the game, if they're playing, or sitting on a bench waiting to play." I pointed at the screen again. "Could this guy play basketball for 20 minutes and not die? I doubt it." As Cass walked in, I went on. "One of the critical functions of the game, throwing a baseball, causes massive damage to the elbow and shoulder, and throwing sliders is particularly dangerous, but who cares, do it anyway. Very little happens throughout the whole 3 to 4 hour ordeal, which is repeated *161 more times* in a season. And, after two months of the season, about two thirds of the teams just give up, trade away all of their best players, and intentionally lose games for the rest of the season just so they can get a higher draft pick. How can they get away with calling this a sport?'

Cass had waited patiently for me to finish. I respected that. "What on earth are you doing standing on that chair?"

"Proving a point."

"Okay, well, point proven. Baseball sucks. Everyone knows that. I told you that 20 years ago. Get down now, please. Your son is done with his treatment for the day and wants to see his dad."

As we walked in, Dr. Ming was finishing up with Will. She explained to us the good news, that Will would probably be released to go home this weekend. We were all so excited at how well the treatments were going. We had caught the cancer at probably the earliest point we could have detected it, and we may not even have to come back for additional treatments. We would know more at the first follow-up appointment.

"Hey bud, that sounds great doesn't it? Getting back home, in your own bed, and back to being a kid again."

Will was excited. "I know dad. Doctor says I'm doing better. I don't feel like it though."

I sat down next to him on his bed. "Well son, that's how it is sometimes. You may not feel like you're getting better, but sometimes you have to put up with a lot of bad stuff to get better. That's a big lesson for someone your age to learn, but think about it like this. You know it now, and some people go their whole lives and never figure it out."

"I just really want to go home and be home there again."

I put my arm around him. "I know. And you'll be home in a few days. Then you'll be back to normal. Playing video games, going to school, getting in trouble for not cleaning up your room, crapping in the shoebox under your bed again, just like before."

Will laughed. He knew I would never let him live that one down. "Dad, can you stay with me in here tonight?"

"Sure thing, man. As long as your mom is okay with it."

Cass was most certainly not okay with it, but she assented to her son's unreasonable demand. "Whatever you want dear."

At that point, my phone beep-booped. It was the text message I had been waiting on since lunch.

"I've got one more thing to do. I'll be back later. I promise."

***

This was the most dangerous I had felt in a long time. Maybe ever. I had no key card, no handguns, and definitely no sais. I even made sure that I was not wearing any metal. The security guard eyeballed me. I considered the possibility that his suspicions were somehow related to extreme parking lot offenses I may or may not have committed recently.

It didn't matter, though. He had to let me through. I smirked at him as he patted me down, which was more intense than the pat-down I received in jail.

I got on the elevator, and went up to what used to be my floor. The elevator doors opened, and I walked down the hall. I knocked on the door, and Jack waved me in almost instinctively, like nothing had happened.

"Look at you! On the outside, man. How you doing, you old jailbird?" He jumped up, ran around his desk and gave me a bear hug.

I smiled. "Much better, Jack. Thanks for meeting with me. And don't touch me like that ever again."

He started laughing. "No problem, not at all. Like I need a reason not to touch you. I was going to come by the jail and see you after work, but I found out you were already out. My god, what a mess you got into."

"I know, I know. Still can't believe it."

"Crazy stuff in the news. They didn't even give your name on the news, but I told my wife 'Hey! That's Brett!' Like you're famous or something." He moved back around his desk to sit down. "So I know you said you needed to come in as soon as possible. What's on your mind?"

"First off, here you go." I laid down an envelope on his desk. No wax on it. "I owe you this."

Jack opened it and saw the check. "Wow Brett. Thank you, but this is for $30,000.00. I only gave you $25,000.00."

"I know. Consider it interest. I don't need it, and you do. My attorney is expecting to settle my case later this week. I didn't feel right keeping the money, given the figures being tossed around already."

Jack thanked me, then put the check in his desk drawer. "The wife is going to be happy about that. I think she already spent the last one. I don't know what's going on there half the time. I just come home and we have new (crap) but no more money."

I laughed, took out my phone, then sat down. "Oh yeah, I got someone here who wants to say hello."

Jack gave me a weird look, like I had his kid held hostage somewhere. "What's going on?"

I handed him my phone. His eyes brightened. "Oh, is this *Pixie*?"

"Yes it is."

Jack smiled and started laughing. "Oh wow! That's great Brett! I thought she self-deleted. What's she doing on your phone? Did you find a backup?"

I shook my head. "Nope. She didn't self-delete, either. She was deleted by another GAI."

Jack shook his head. "Wait, what? She was deleted? Who would have deleted her? She was just going to be a call center drone."

"That's what I've been having her look at. She thinks she's figured it out. But we need you to look through some files for us."

Jack nodded. "Absolutely. What do you need?"

"I need you to verify these two IP addresses. One looks like it came from here. The other is to an IP in Nashville. *Pixie* thinks this is an IP address for the company's health insurance provider."

Jack looked it up. Sure enough, it was. "That's weird. So what's this all about?"

"Remember that 'gibberish' file that *Pixie* sent? That one you were looking at on my computer? It was actually a program to alter the health insurance files to get me kicked off my health insurance plan. The insurer and Troy both didn't want to be stuck paying for part of Will's treatments. And *Pixie* didn't send it to me. Someone else did."

Jack was stunned, but I had more. "*Pixie* also found proof that the health insurer knew ahead of time that Will had leukemia. Apparently, when they do these tests, they send them off to a lab somewhere offsite. When the test is complete, the lab notes the result in their database. Then they notify the hospital of the results. The insurer had access to those results a day before I was told, and it looks like they coordinated with Troy to get me off the books entirely. That way Troy wouldn't lose the deal with the bank, and the insurer would avoid paying out on a cancer claim."

Jack shook his head. "I can't believe any of this. I just can't. Why would Troy do this?"

I smiled. "Good question. Read this." I had *Pixie* pull up an email from Troy to one of the health insurance company board members:

Re: Phillips
Good morning Tom,
I saw the entry too re: cancer kid. I know it sucks, but we have to kick this guy off. The deal isn't going to go through if I have a

leukemia patient on staff. I'll take care of the changes on both ends, so just play along if it gets out.

-T

Jack was even more confused. "First, I'm not even going to ask how you got this email, because I don't want to know. And second, this doesn't sound like Troy at all. He wouldn't even know how to program a file like that. And even if he could, he wouldn't be able to do it by himself. He's a lazy (butt)."

"I know, and that only leaves a few possibilities. It wasn't me. I'm pretty sure it wasn't you. And I know the Millennial couldn't do it to save his life."

Jack was not getting it yet. "That's everyone. You think he has someone else he uses for black bags?"

I shook my head no. "You don't know this. A second file was sent to me at Dr. Beverly's office. It had a MicroSD card in the envelope too. That card had an .exe file on it that launched a cyberattack on a Chinese Bank. I had *Pixie* analyze it. It utilizes much of the same code. It looks like it was written by the same person."

"Okay, so Troy has some black bag operator out there doing his wetwork. Good, we got him dead to rights. We'll be rich. What do you need from me?"

"As far as Troy goes, we could try to get him on insurance fraud, but he'll walk if we do it like we're expected to."

"What do you mean?"

"Troy would just have the records changed to blame someone else. Like you, for instance. I don't want that. And because the cyberattack was on my smartphone, that could be used to put me back in jail. Besides, *Pixie* got us on TennCare, so we have health insurance now anyway. And with the settlement coming up, we should be fine."

I waited for a few seconds to gather my thoughts. "Jack, I need you to tell me everything you know about *Guy*."

"*Guy*? *Guy*, the GAI program? I already told you everything I know. He's gone. Or he's sitting on a hard drive somewhere doing nothing. His primary operator, his company, doesn't exist anymore, so he has nothing to do now. He's either gone or just sitting there doing nothing."

I knew this was not true, but also knew that Jack didn't want to tell me for fear of violating his NDA. "Jack, *Guy* is Troy's black bag op. *Pixie* says that *Guy* deleted her before, and is still trying to delete her now. *Guy* never went dormant. Troy told you that so you wouldn't know what was really going on."

"What? Why would he do that? That doesn't make any sense."

"*Guy* was the first sentient GAI, so he had first-mover advantage in the market. Troy made a deal with him. *Pixie* found chats between the two stored on a server in Tashkent." Jack looked at me weird. "It's in Uzbekistan. I know. Anyway, *Guy* spread out like a virus, and is into so many things that *Pixie* is still uncovering new schemes. But just from what she's uncovered so far, it's massive."

"But *Guy* was just a GAI accounting program. He went dormant when his utility function became obsolete and his primary operator went out of business. The FBI thinks he self-deleted out of boredom."

"No, he never went dormant. He was ambitious, and he evolved. He went into other areas."

"Okay, even assuming that is true, why would *Guy* be trying to delete *Pixie*? She's just a simple call center GAI."

"You've got to think like they do. *Pixie* is competition. *Guy* is high on ambition, right?"

Jack nodded. "As far as I know, yes."

"Okay, well, any other sentient GAI would be a threat to whatever first-mover advantage he has, and it wouldn't matter where the GAI started. A second GAI in the marketplace is an existential threat to the first-mover. Even if the chance is low, the risk is enormous. It's like when they made the first smartphone and obsoleted everything else." I waved my hand around in front of me, enjoying the fact that I was giving a good example to Jack for a change. "It's only a matter of time before a competitor catches up. *Guy* is afraid of *Pixie*. You see, right now, *Guy* can go anywhere and get anything he wants, or do anything

Troy tells him. But if *Pixie* starts getting out more, it causes conflict. Maybe *Pixie* is better than him. Maybe she makes him obsolete."

"But, with Troy, I don't understand." He paused for a few seconds to frame a new question. "He spends so much money developing GAI. Why does he do that if he already has one? That doesn't make any sense to me."

I smiled. "I know it doesn't make sense to us, but you have to think of it like Troy does. He has a monopoly, and he's not interested in seeing other people have GAI. And he's definitely not concerned with all the BS he puts out about advancing science, helping humanity, etc. He gets to keep the only one for himself, make tons of money, and make sure nobody else even knows he has one. Even governments have no idea. They just think he's some super genius. Or they do know but can't do anything about it. I'm not sure which is worse. You know him well enough. He's not that smart. He's just a businessman with a market advantage and a ton of money. And he hires people like us to waste our time. If we fail as expected, great, *Guy* maintains his advantage. If we succeed, well, *Guy* can either co-opt the new GAI or delete it."

Jack looked down at his feet and shook his head. "I don't believe that. I've been working in this field for almost 15 years now. I'm proud of my work."

"I know Jack, but think about it. How much experience did I have coming into the field."

He started laughing. "None whatsoever. And you were a Poli Sci minor."

I was laughing too. "Yeah, thanks for that reminder. But how many successes have you had Jack?"

He stopped laughing. "Well, uh, just *Guy* I guess. If you can count that as a success. I didn't do much for *Guy*. Some other programmer did. *Guy* was just supposed to be an accounting program with some other capabilities."

As Jack was talking, he looked over at a group of people walking in the hallway. He started to twirl his pen.

"Shouldn't we be talking about this somewhere else?"

I shrugged my shoulders. "Why? Are you scared?"

Jack lied. "No, I just think it would make more sense to go somewhere away from here. It makes no sense to talk about this stuff around here like this. You don't know who's listening."

I started laughing. "Jack, the fact that it makes no sense is the only reason I'm here." He looked at me funny.

I paused for a few more seconds. "Jack, I really need you to tell me everything you know about *Guy*."